The Image of Blood

The Golden Blade 1996

The Image of Blood

The Golden Blade No. 48

Edited by William Forward
and Andrew Wolpert

Floris Books

First published in 1995 by Floris Books.

© 1995 Floris Books, Edinburgh
All rights reserved. No part of this publication may be reproduced without the prior permission of Floris Books, 15 Harrison Gardens, Edinburgh.

British Library CIP Data available

ISBN 0-86315-224-4
ISSN 0967-6708

Printed in Great Britain
by Redwood Books, Trowbridge, Wilts.

Anthroposophy springs from the work and teaching of Rudolf Steiner (1861-1925). He describes it as a 'path of knowledge, to guide the spiritual in the human being to the spiritual in the universe.'

The aim of this yearly journal is to bring the outlook of anthroposophy to bear on questions and activities of evident relevance to the present, in a way which may have a lasting value. It was founded in 1949 by Charles Davy and Arnold Freeman, who were its first editors.

The title derives from an old Persian legend, according to which King Djemjdid received from his god, Ahura Mazdao, a golden blade with which to fulfil his mission on earth. It carried the heavenly forces of light into the darkness of earthly substance, thus allowing its transformation. The legend points to the possibility that humanity, through wise and compassionate work with the earth, can one day regain on a new level what was lost when the Age of Gold was supplanted by those of Silver, Bronze and Iron. Technology could serve this aim; instead of endangering our planet's life, it could help to make the earth a new sun.

Contents

Editorial notes	9
The Mystery of the Blood *James Dyson*	13
The Bleeding Wound of King Amfortas *Karal Jan Tusenius*	43
D.H. Lawrence's *The Rainbow*, the Lion, and the Blood of Sophia *Andrew Welburn*	55
Mithras, the Bull, and the Transformation of the Blood *Christopher Clouder*	73
Of Blood and Money *Christopher Houghton Budd*	85
Money — the Christ-Blood of the Threefold Social Order *Jack Foster*	93
Chosen Destiny *Rudi Lissau*	105
Book reviews *Jenny Josephson*	121
Notes on the contributors	125

Editorial notes

Medical science acknowledges that a consciously nurtured sense of self-esteem is a significant factor in reducing the likelihood of HIV patients developing AIDS-related illnesses. This attests to a connection between the individual ego and the blood. It is this relationship that provides the context for this issue of *The Golden Blade*.

An image arises out of intuitive and inspired concepts and adds a dimension to what is visible: an image also serves as a symbolic manifestation of what is invisible. The image of blood is formed not only out of cumulative cultural connotations, but also as a revelation of the spiritual activity that manifests in microscopically visible and chemically analyzable processes. Such physiological dynamics of metamorphosis and exchange are themselves images of transformation in a wider evolutionary sense.

The culturally universal significance of blood in rituals sacred and profane, and all the attendant emotive connotations of love, murder, kinship and sacrifice, achieve a particular messianic climax in the Christian tradition: the flowing into the earth of the redemptive blood on Golgotha. In connection with this evolutionary event for the whole of humanity, Rudolf Steiner relates the forces of the ego through the blood to the possibility of individual transformation. Among the exercises he describes for awakening dormant soul faculties is the rose-cross meditation. The preparation for this, as outlined in Chapter 5 of *Occult Science,* consists of imagining the comparison between plant sap and human blood. We know that a red rose is the result of unimpassioned growth forces, and discover that it can become a symbol of what blossoms in the human soul when the impulses and passions associated with the blood are purified. This purification is not an obedient monastic repression, but a freely willed permeation with consciousness.

Both James Dyson and Karal Tusenius, from their medical and biochemical perspective, characterize the blood in relation to identity and the ego. Both also provide explicit connections to the Grail theme of our last issue. The first article takes the themes of transubstantiation and resurrection in the blood as an introduction to the substance of antimony and the process of coagulation. The redemptive possibilities of the blood lead to questions of karma, and the image that the Holy Grail gives form to substance.

In Karal Tusenius' article, the mobility, versatility, and literally metaphysical properties of the blood shines through the detailed chemistry, and the biographical significance of illness brings our attention again to Parsifal and Amfortas. James Dyson's closing evocation of the rainbow, points us towards Andrew Welburn's opening images from D.H. Lawrence, and the powerful apocalyptic and gnostic imagination of "meeting the lion."

In Christopher Clouder's article, Mithras seen as the precursor of Christ, where the fertilizing blood prefigures the redeeming blood, is the context in which we are reminded of the details of Crucifixions from the early Middle Ages. The connection between ego and blood was known to Raphael, whose *Crucifixion* in the National Gallery in London bears his name, the conscious sign of his individuality, in just that place at the foot of the Cross where the earlier iconography had traditionally depicted the blood entering the earth. Clouder leads us to consider how Raphael further transformed this in his *Madonna del Prato* painting in Vienna.

A particular connection in the last three articles arises for me out of their relevance to Shakespeare's *The Merchant of Venice*. The obvious comparison of blood and money stimulates Christopher Budd to explore the simile of expansion and contraction. What truly distinguishes Shylock from Antonio is the fact that Antonio's money circulates openly and stimulates more than just economic activity, whereas Shylock's wealth is furtively "coagulated" (and invites theft!). Well may one wonder why Shylock craves Antonio's heart. The Christians in this play fall far short of the compassion and forgiveness which live in the heart of the faith that so gratifyingly separates them from the Jew. But their faults must not serve to eclipse Shylock's, and neither should we mistake Shylock's much quoted speech that includes the line "if you prick us do we not bleed?" It is precisely the image of blood and money that leads us beyond instinctive partisanship and seductive questions of anti-semitism. The symbolism of the blood in this play transcends our emotional or politically correct reactions and reveals that both Shylock and Antonio yearn for their as yet unattained humanity. This common, and most human quality (that Shylock is not yet able to articulate in his list of comparable attributes) is a brotherhood that comes not from consanguinity. It arises from the transforming ego activity for which the blood provides the instrument and the ingredients. Rudolf Steiner describes the morality of this microcosmic task in his lecture "The Etherization of the Blood" (October 1, 1911), and speaks of how the human bloodstream unites with the macrocosmic bloodstream of Christ. The esoteric economic transubstantiation of the earth gives Jack Foster the explicitly Christian motive that continues to challenge us in Shakespeare's play. Finally the question of "chosen destiny" that Rudi Lissau addresses is deeply connected to the blood theme so provocatively represented by Shylock.

The alchemy from which each of us can distil our own approach to Rudi Lissau's theme could well begin in the crucible combining the insights of all these contributors. I dare to imagine that the most un-Christian forced impoverishment and conversion of Shylock are a mocking parody that can be redeemed only by the transubstantiation effected through a freely chosen deed of incarnation. In our ego-conscious participation in the redemptive process, the blood we choose to inherit is both the means and the matter.

A.W.

The Mystery of the Blood

James Dyson

"Blood is a very special fluid." Steiner often refers to this saying of Goethe's. In which respects can we see blood as a very special fluid? If we simply look at what is obvious about the blood, what we know about it, we see that it just about exists in the world of space, but is, however, primarily an organ which exists in time, continually changing, continually moving, adapting itself to the various conditions which prevail in the different organs.

There is, however, a part of the blood, a certain fraction of its protein content, which is constant. It is, of course, continually being created and destroyed, as indeed are all the tissues and organs in the body. In that respect it is continually forming and dissolving, as indeed are the bones. But at least in its healthy state this part of the blood stays put within the actual blood vessels — that is to say, it isn't continually moving backwards and forwards between capillaries and tissue fluid. It remains at any one time intact, forming a more or less cohesive whole within the blood circulation. That means to say that it stays within the boundaries of those blood vessels which are at their most expanded within the heart and at their most contracted within the periphery of the body, in the capillaries. This component of the blood, which is formed from high molecular weight protein, represents only a relatively small part of the totality of the blood, approximately between 5–10%. Apart from the red blood cells, which I will return to later, every other component of the blood is continually in a kind of dynamic interplay between the various organs and tissue fluid throughout the entire human body. Apart from this very small fraction, the blood as a whole permeates the entire living organism, and if one asks the question: "What does it contain, what is it made of?" — the answer would have to be: "Everything that is to be found anywhere at all within the human organism."

If, to begin with, we call to mind the three main groups of organic substances — carbohydrates, fats and proteins — we note they are all to be found within the blood. It is well known that fats are in the blood; there is a great deal of talk these days about cholesterol and fatty deposits and so on. Similarly, carbohydrates are in the blood; you need only bring to mind glucose; if glucose levels are not properly regulated we become unconscious. I have already mentioned that part of the blood which is structural and which is composed of high molecular weight protein. In addition to this, however, all the intermediary metabolic products of protein synthesis, the amino-acids, polypeptides and so on, which are elaborated further into organic structures in the various organs, these are also part of the blood. This dynamic interplay between blood and body also includes every mineral that we find in the blood. As a doctor, one thinks first of all of sodium and potassium, and then perhaps of calcium and phosphate — these are the more obvious ones. The dynamic equilibrium between sodium and potassium in the blood and in the tissue fluid, and indeed between these substances in the tissue fluid and inside the actual cells of the body, is one of the most finely regulated and important so-called homeostatic mechanisms, but in fact it isn't a mechanism at all! It would be far better to describe it as an ecological relationship. Within homeostasis a slight irregularity in the relationship between blood and cell of any one of these minerals can make all the difference between life and death. Calcium, similarly, is in a continual dynamic interplay between the blood and the bone. And this is not merely a passive state of equilibrium. It depends on physiological activity which varies from one moment to the next. It changes, albeit only minimally, even with walking and sleeping, but it changes much more radically if we are confined to bed for a period of time. It also changes to a marked degree between youth and old age, and even with changes in respiration and nutritional status, as well as in countless different kinds of illnesses. These processes all involve, amongst other things, hormonal activity — and hormones are also particular examples of proteins which are continually being secreted into the blood stream by the endocrine glands; immunoglobulins are also proteins.

At every moment, a profoundly important balance is maintained in relation to the concentration of literally every mineral in the blood. And this, of course, includes the metals. In all probability, every single metal, certainly the seven main metals, are involved in some form or other either as co-enzymes or catalysts, for certain biochemical processes in the body. When Steiner spoke about metals, the only one that was known to be important within the body in any substantial amount, was iron, which occupies such a central role within the haemoglobin of the red blood cells. But lead, tin, gold, silver, mercury, copper, most if not all of them are now known to play a vital part within the body's metabolism as trace elements. We know how much emphasis is placed these days in some circles on diagnosing conditions such as zinc or magnesium deficiency. The health food trade stresses, amongst other things, an awareness of the body's need for trace elements and metals. And yet, in the amounts in which these are normally dispensed, certain questions may arise. The body requires only the minutest traces of many of these substances. The physiological levels of most trace elements in the body correspond to homeopathic potency ranges of between D4 and D15. I suspect that some trace elements are active in even higher dilutions than this.

The chemistry of these substances as they occur in the natural world is, of course, very well known, but when you are considering how trace elements behave in the body, it is necessary to form quite a different mental image of the substance and even of its chemical activity, from the one which we have transposed from our ordinary knowledge of how the substance behaves in outer nature. One of the maxims that occurs over and over again in all Steiner's medical lectures, is that "substances are processes, processes substances." This expresses itself in the fact that in the body these substances are mainly catalytic in one or other biochemical pathway. The substance itself is not exerting that kind of chemical action which it would in the test tube, but it is facilitating a biological reaction and thereby revealing something of its own inner affinities which can only be expressed within living systems. The blood is that organ through which all these substance processes are interconnected, mediated, held in a condition of openness to influences of temperature, pressure, hormonal variations and much else of a more subtle, ever cosmic nature.

These things are, of course, elaborated in much greater depth in courses on physiology. Let us, however, move on and briefly consider the cells of the blood. The blood is also a living organ in its own right; it is not only a fluid in which minerals, carbohydrates, proteins, lipids and so on exist in a dynamic interplay with the body, it is itself alive in so far as it has a cellular structure. Historically, three broad divisions have been described among the cells of the blood; the so-called red cells, the so-called white cells and the platelets. This was already known when Rudolf Steiner was speaking about the blood. The platelets had, however, been identified only recently in his time and in a way they occupy a very special place historically within anthroposophical experimental physiology. They were the subject of study of Lily Kolisko. I am not sure how to interpret her findings in the context of current knowledge, but they were certainly relevant in their time and in some way probably still are. She was perhaps the first person to look through the microscope with the eye of the spiritual scientist. And this represented quite a landmark within the history of anthroposophy altogether.

We mustn't forget that anthroposophy grew and developed, in the first instance, within a theosophical soil. And theosophy wasn't so very concerned about investigating and understanding the world of outer nature — it was far more concerned about elaborating pictures of the human being, but in a purely spiritual sense. This call from Rudolf Steiner to connect spiritual understanding with sense perceptions and thereby build a new spiritual science arising from these sense impressions — this call, which intensified as the years passed by, was finally taken up by Lily Kolisko, in her physiological study of platelets and the spleen. I think it was the gesture of her endeavours, even more than their final conclusions, which evoked Steiner's enthusiasm. Indeed, he spoke with unreserved positivity and warmth about her work. What is, of course, now established — I am not sure to what extent it was at the time — is that platelets contribute to what we now call the process of blood coagulation. Whenever we are injured, even in a very minor way, these minute entities form a kind of plug in the injured tissues and around this basis the thrombus or clot forms, thereby preventing further bleeding and insulating the body from potential invasion by infective micro-organisms. The injury becomes, in the first instance, sealed off by this platelet plug. The platelets therefore exercise a kind of protective function within the blood, and around the plug of platelets a complementary process of blood coagulation takes place which is one of the most fundamental homeostatic processes of healing. To anticipate a little Grail imagery, we may at this point ask what it means when the wound doesn't heal; the wound that doesn't stop bleeding may in a way have to do with a failure in this process of blood coagulation. A very deep mystery belongs to this process and I am sure one could also explore this mystery in relation to the hidden activities with which the spleen is connected.

Be that as it may, the platelets are a kind of débris or

residue of very much larger blood cells called megakaryocytes. These cells are generated in the bone marrow and are very large cells which break down into hundreds of minute particles, which are then dispersed in the blood in the form of platelets. By the time they have evolved to the stage of being platelets, they have already died in the primary cellular form, but their origin is cellular and they are therefore closely connected to the realm of life. They are, however, the furthest removed from life of all the cellular components within the blood.

If we now move on to the red blood cells, they are one step nearer to life than the platelets. As a cell, they are just about intact, in so far as they retain a cell membrane and are able to breathe a little, but essentially their internal physiology has already come to an end. In health they have lost their nucleus by the time they enter the blood circulation from the bone marrow — the nucleus is that part of the cell which is essential if protein synthesis and cell division are to continue in an active way. The red cells have essentially sacrificed their life, yet they carry on functioning in a certain respect. They are the only cells in the body which have died and which are not straightaway either excreted or internally metabolized because they have died. They are remarkable structures, because they remain in the body in a state of suspended animation, being allotted on average something like 120 days of grace in this state, in which they may go on functioning within the blood. Their functions include carrying haemoglobin, the pigmented substance that gives the blood its red colour and combines with the oxygen in the lungs as one of the main gases involved in the processes of cellular respiration.

How is it possible that these almost dead entities can remain part of a living organism that would normally eliminate anything dead straight away? The answer to this question is almost certainly to be found in connection with the mystery of iron, because these red blood cells have become the carriers of iron via the protein haemoglobin. Its internal configuration is such that the iron substance is taken out of the realm of weight and brought into a relationship to the surrounding fluid which is comparable to a kind of colloidal relationship. A colloid is the name given to a state of matter in which substance in one form, for example water, becomes interpenetrated with substance in another form, for example oil. The chemical process whereby iron is bound within the haemoglobin is called chelation. It is a very remarkable type of bonding, whereby substances bind together in such a way that the iron is encapsulated in a protein molecule, and through the laws of physical chemistry that prevail at such minute dimension levels, the iron is rendered almost entirely weightless. This process could also be imagined as bringing the iron into a condition in which it is sensitive to cosmic supersensible influences. Once again, the phrase "suspended animation" comes to mind. We can carry within our blood, quite literally, several grams of iron, but through the subtle chemistry at work in the haemoglobin it is rendered virtually weightless. This must, I believe, be connected in some mysterious way to the remarkable fact that the red blood cells retain their ability to remain alive, as it were, after the moment of their biological death.

Steiner has said much about the mission of iron within the human organism and about the fact that the incorporation of iron into the human organism is among the most significant of all physiological facts. It is deeply connected with a kind of archetypal healing which took place after the Fall of Man. If you bring together these statements and what I have just described regarding the presence of iron within these almost dead red blood cells, something may inwardly resonate in your souls. Within each of these red cells the iron prevents a death process which then allows the entire organism to continue to live through carrying the process of oxygen into the depths of the organism. Without this the possibility of the cells to breathe and respire would have been lost in Lemuria and Atlantis, when the human being separated off from the divine world, from that state of being in which, at that time, substance and process were still totally united. Before the Fall, substance came into existence but disappeared again from existence. Materialization and de-materialization were continually taking place. After the Fall, more substance appeared than was able to be absorbed back into its original state. More substance precipitated from the realm of being, from the realm of eternity, into the realm of space and remained caught, stuck, locked, imprisoned in space. The incorporation of the iron into our bodily substance enabled life to continue nevertheless, but only for just long enough for the ego to have a single incarnation. The iron has, you might say, bought us the time for our earthly incarnation, just as it has bought each red cell these 120 days of suspended animation. We can see this when we realize that this iron pigment, this haemoglobin, is the essential vehicle for the transport of oxygen in the blood, through which a perpetual process of dying is partially counteracted.

Haemoglobin is also deeply connected with the transport of carbon dioxide. Its relationship to oxygen is a very obvious one and very well known, because the oxygenated haemoglobin gives to the arterial blood its bright red colour; de-oxygenated haemoglobin is the much darker, magenta blue of venous blood. But also within and closely connected to the haemoglobin are enzymatic processes and cellular buffers — that is to say, physiological processes which govern and regulate, at a very subtle level, acid base balance in the blood. They regulate and are part of the internal ecology of carbon dioxide metabolism.

Variation in blood carbon dioxide levels are, from a certain point of view, even more important than variations in oxygen levels. This fact is now commonly recognized and thought in some circles to contribute to many of the modern and recently studied illnesses, such as coronary artery disease and chronic fatigue syndrome (the so-called ME). When, for whatever reason, but often through some form of anxiety state, perhaps carried even at an unconscious level over many years, one breathes too fast and too shallowly, the carbon dioxide levels of the blood become thereby depleted. The body can compensate for this to some extent but, over a very long period of time, resulting disturbances in acid base balance and other biochemical processes may lead to physical changes in, amongst other things, fat and calcium deposition. Indeed, while it is easy to over-exhale the carbon dioxide, it is different regarding over-inhaling of oxygen. However hard and fast we breath, the actual oxygen within the haemoglobin of the blood soon reaches a kind of plateau and however much one may try, one can't inhale more, because the internal system is saturated. But the same isn't true of carbon dioxide. One can deplete that very considerably through hyperventilation. If we follow through some of Rudolf Steiner's statements regarding the relationship between these two gases in the blood we are confronted with remarkable images that touch on the deeper secrets of waking and sleeping and of conscious intentionality and karma, of the continual battle between these two currents in our lives. Each individual red blood cell, in so far as it is continually suffering and balancing out this relationship between carbon dioxide and oxygen, is at the same time the physical basis of that polarity in the body that exists between the conscious life of will and the unconscious life of will. Carbon dioxide levels tend to rise when we are asleep; they are connected to those processes which take place under the guidance of the spiritual beings of the higher hierarchies which work into the human body at night, in the place of our conscious ego and astral body.

In this polarity between the conscious and unconscious life of the will, the mystery between what we carry at a pre-earthly level as potential karma and that conscious activity whereby we either do or do not convert that potential into actual deed, comes to expression. The conversion of potential into deed belongs essentially to the iron principle and to waking day consciousness. But the guardianship of the pre-earthly spiritual potentiality or intentionality lives in that other pole of night consciousness. One can begin to see why so many modern illnesses which are bound up with sleeplessness and carbon dioxide depletion, may be connected with the tendency for the conscious life to be deflected away from the pre-earthly intention. The treatment of such illnesses may, amongst other things, have to include the dawning understanding that the need to be in control is part of the illness-producing process. The possibility to let go or hand control over to a higher reality, often belongs to the gateway to healing. I am aware that this may sound paradoxical at first hearing. Such a step may, however, have a profound effect on the breathing, of course over a period of time, and thereby the carbon dioxide levels of the blood may change and the balance between upbuilding processes and processes of demolition be once again favourably restored.

Before moving on from the subject of blood gases, I should say that I am aware that I have only made the first tentative approach to the complex question of how carbon dioxide and oxygen levels are connected to these more subtle relationships between waking and sleeping, and the related physiological processes of anabolism and catabolism.

I was attempting to enumerate the different substances in the blood, and am still only half way through the cells! In addition to its connection to the transport of gases, Steiner also connects the red blood cells to the phosphorus "substance process." The importance of the biochemistry of phosphorus in relation to the storage and release of energy used in movement, has become well known since Steiner's time. Broadly speaking, phosphorus exists in a bound form in which its energy remains hidden in the realm of potential and in a free form after the energy has been released. In the fifth lecture of Steiner's second cycle to doctors, recently published in English under the title "Anthroposophical Spiritual Scientific and Medical Therapy," we are given an image of the red blood cells as a kind of organ of breathing in their own right, holding the balance between the free and the bound phosphorus, between energy that is realized through a spiritualized process of combustion and energy which is held back as potential.

Let us now move on to the white cells. Very little was known about these cells in Steiner's lifetime. It was known that one type, belonging to this group, the so-called neutrophils or granulocytes — cells with large and rather complicated shaped nuclei — had to do with defence against bacteria. They were known to be phagocytic, which simply means that they eat things up, particularly foreign organisms that shouldn't be there. Phagocytosis is derived from the Greek word which means "eating up." These are cells which digest, and whenever we have a small infection in the skin and pus comes out, that pus is, at least to a very large extent, the dead, broken down cell bodies of these particular white cells which have sacrificed themselves in the process of dealing with the foreigners in order to protect the integrity of the inner space of human immunity. All this was known, at least in broad outline, in Steiner's time, but the role of that group of cells which we nowadays call lymphocytes and which also belong to the white cell population, was still largely a mystery. They were hardly known or understood at all at that time. Probably more knowledge has accumulated in the last thirty-five years around just this type of cell, than any other cell in the body. Even as little as thirty-five years ago, not so very much more had been discovered than in Steiner's day.

In the late sixties when I first started at medical school, the saga of the lymphocyte was just beginning to unfold. And this saga was really quite something to study! Nowadays it has become ten or even twenty volumes thick, and there are professorial chairs that deal with just parts of it. What I am of course speaking of is the history of immunology. These cells are, in a way, the heart of that activity whereby the human being maintains its physiological integrity, its separateness from the outside world. From what one picks up nowadays, for instance about immune deficiency, just through press and communications media, one can almost assume a kind of general level of knowledge in this realm. There is, however, an enormous differentiation of function among the lymphocytes, and these cells work in close collaboration with other cells called monocytes or macrophages. They have many different groups of sub-populations differentiated just like a garrison in defence of the outside world. Some cells have to do with sounding the alert that something is on the way in and other cells have to do with conveying that message to so-called headquarters. In turn others have to do with going back from headquarters to other sub-depots that can unite sub-garrisons of troops which then rise up and hopefully enter the blood and deal with the invasion. This is the kind of language of imagery which one meets nowadays in the popular press, at the level of immunology. Other cells are also involved, which I have not mentioned, but which broadly speaking serve a related function.

One can't describe the blood without approaching this remarkable saga of "self" and "non-self," this remarkable mystery of our own absolute physiological uniqueness, which in its very language is highly suggestive of the ego struggling at a psychological level to uphold its own identity in an unfavourable climate.

The closer one comes to the human being in the conventionally understood sense of the phylogenetic progression, that is to say, starting with the invertebrates and moving through the vertebrates to the lower and higher mammals, the more one finds individual specificity in the immune system. It is only in the human being, however, that this is fully established in relation to each single person. This "own identity" of ours is, I would suggest, the physiological basis for that part of us which is also utterly unique, namely our karma. As spiritual beings, I suspect that we are not really unique at all. What we have brought forward with us as human beings from Old Saturn, Old Sun and Old Moon, and to which ego substance has been added on this earth, is really something universal in which we are united together. I am not for one moment wanting to imply that spiritual individuality does not exist, but only that what confers upon each of us our uniqueness is what we call our individual karma. Each one of us is making totally unique experiences that can never be repeated or replicated yet which belong absolutely and uniquely, as a single fragment, within the totality of the ego substance which was originally our common possession. That individual karmic essence has its physiological basis, I believe, within our immune system.

It is possible to study the various immunologically active cells in the blood in a Goetheanistic way, and to discover within them polarities of structure and function. All I can do now is to point to the fact that when such terms as granulocytes, lymphocytes, monocytes and so on fall from our tongue, they conceal some of the deepest mysteries of human existence and they guard the very foundations of our earthly life and destiny.

Something of this was already more than just hinted at — indeed it was quite distinctly described — by Steiner towards the end of his lecture "The Work of the Angels in the Astral Body," where he refers to degenerative diseases of the blood which are likely to appear in the relatively near future, if our own ego doesn't learn how to co-operate with its angel in waking day consciousness. What does that mean? The angel is the guardian of our karma, it is the angel being who accompanies us from life to life. The angel is the being entrusted by the higher hierarchies to look after the individual ego fragment in its time between death and rebirth in such a way that it isn't totally dispersed into the cosmic void, but can be guided back as an integrated being to a new earthly life.

This co-operation with the angel could also be described as an awakening at a conscious level to our unique pre-earthly intention, that which really does distinguish us from other human beings. Without the conscious cooperation with our angel being, it will not be possible as humankind to find a way forward into the future, even physiologically. Our angel will then be forced to work into the etheric body, which is the bearer of those instincts which have to do with our desire nature. This of course came about as a consequence of the Fall, when the realm of matter and space came into being. These instincts, far from leading one into the realm of really meeting and acknowledging one's own karma, lead one into that realm which binds one to the forces of the earth, of which Ahriman is now the ruling lord. Ahriman's main intention is to prevent human karma from working.

Now we know that even this work of the angel as a guardian of human karma is not any longer quite such a straightforward matter as it used to be, even in the relatively recent past. Even this guardianship is now threatened. It is no longer always possible for the individual angel to be the guardian of the karma of the individual human being, and therefore, in consequence, chaos and formlessness are already entering into the human condition. The possibility for the karmic consequences of deeds in one life to find their continuation in the next life, is increasingly threatened. It would only continue in the long run in so far as in our waking day consciousness we have already begun to identify ourselves with our angel, otherwise after death the human soul may be bound to the earthly sphere and be unable to continue its journey through the planetary realms in which new karma is formed in accordance with divine guidance. The fragments of the ego which remain bound to the earth then enter the sphere of the Azuric beings whose task is the de-spiritualization of the human ego. Even certain so-called medicines may contribute towards this ego fragmentation and of course questions arise around all aspects of substance-abuse and organ transplantation.

These things — and more — are hinted at in the lecture "The Work of the Angels in the Astral Body." Steiner connects these developments quite directly to degenerative changes in the blood, which may well be those which are now emerging and which are described as disorders of immunity of various kinds — including immune deficiency states. In considering such conditions — for example so-called HIV infections — we must be careful never to form moral judgements in relation to the sick person. Illnesses may be an expression of individual karma, but can also be connected to the social karma of a particular community of human beings or even to the wider aspect of world karma. Someone may take on the destiny of an illness just because he or she may have the inner potentiality to cope with it and in the long run transform it. In this respect the person may have the role of a kind of "advanced guard." What is at stake is that bodies, in which immunity can still express itself, can be preserved. In so far as this battle doesn't succeed, a new race of human bodies will gradually arise, in many respects closer to the animals than to human beings. This race will not become physiologically distinct in the present epoch of time, but it is already in preparation. The remnants of ego consciousness which such bodies may still retain will be bound to the realm of space and their behaviour will be of a predictable or reflex nature. These beings will be programmed to function very well on an intellectual level, and no doubt they will also retain their instincts and desires, probably in a very crude form. On other levels, however, they will perhaps appear to be quite sophisticated!

Many of the drugs that we use nowadays, which influence our immune system directly or indirectly, are already preparing the way for this. I even include vaccines and antibiotics in this category — which is not to say that it may not sometimes be necessary to use these in medical practice. Steroids, immunosuppressant agents and chemotherapy are more radical examples and a large proportion of the drugs that have been produced since Steiner's lifetime fall into this category. They are, indeed, often life-saving and I am not saying they have no place in medical practice. We cannot be fundamentalistic or fanatical, and must essentially share the karma of our age! But by preventing death, are they perhaps also paving the way for human beings to lose their ability to die in the true sense — thereby becoming fettered to the realm of space and the realm of matter?

I would suggest that the use of such drugs — which are often linked to organ transplantation — will become one of the many ethical crises which medicine will be confronted with at a future point of time. Problems to do with conception and eugenics are at last beginning to have a public and professional airing. Eugenics is concerned with the mysteries of karma in relation to birth, whereas the drugs that I am describing are more connected to the mysteries of death.

Let us for the moment return to the subject of blood coagulation. Although we take it so much for granted, what is actually taking place when the blood clots? In the moment of clotting, time becomes space. The moment of the clot is the moment that something becomes fixed and a focus of precipitation enters into the blood. It is a kind of recapitulation of that which began to take place in the entire human body after the Fall. There is a continuous tension in the blood between the coagulated and the uncoagulated state and in this tension the relationship between time and space finds its expression. It is also connected with the two time streams, that is to say, the upbuilding stream of the etheric body and the destroying stream of the astral body. In relation to this clotting process, Steiner over and over again draws our attention to the substance of antimony. I am so far not aware that orthodox physiology has connected antimony to the clotting process in any way. When I studied blood coagulation it was certainly not the case, but I cannot claim to be fully abreast of the latest discoveries in this field. The process whereby blood clots is one of the most complicated of all the homeostatic or ecological processes in the body — it is a kind of cascade system whereby a chain reaction is set into motion.

Haemophilia is the name of a group of illnesses which are connected with disorders in this blood clotting process. It is very interesting that in the last ten years the problem of haemophilia has become connected with the problem of AIDS — in the sense that some haemophiliacs received blood transfusions which contained the HIV virus before this had been identified. The two illnesses would seem, from all outward considerations, to be totally disconnected, yet the karma of the two conditions has come into a kind of mutual relationship. If you will allow me to make a big jump at this point to the saga of the Grail, I have a kind of suspicion that we may be confronting the nature of Amfortas' illness. Amfortas, you will remember, had received a wound in his groin which would not heal and which was continually bleeding. This wound represented a particular kind of blow of destiny which had a kind of paralysing effect on Amfortas' karma. The problem of Amfortas' wound was that it would not heal — that is to say, the coagulation forces were not strong enough. And it is the antimonizing forces which are weak when the blood cannot clot.

An image which I have found helpful is to compare antimony's relation to the mineral kingdom to that of Viscum or Mistletoe to the plant kingdom — that is to say, both bear within them something of that pre-earthly potential of substance which was not lost at the time of the Fall, and which really belongs to a much earlier stage of evolution. Steiner described the plant Mistletoe as being a remnant of a condition which we left behind on the Old Moon evolution — a condition in which there was an intermediate kingdom between that of the animal and the plant. From that point of view Mistletoe may be described as a kind of "animal-plant," which has retained strongly embryonic characteristics. Similarly, I have often felt that antimony is a kind of living metal, a kind of "plant-mineral." Steiner is continually referring to the plant-like forms and radiating tendencies which it embodies under certain conditions. He describes it as being particularly sensitive to cosmic forces. Perhaps antimony may be considered to be a substance which opens the body at the level of the mineral kingdom to a form — or form principle — which was perhaps built up on Old Saturn and Old Sun. Perhaps this principle is ultimately connected to the physical archetype which can nowadays only be carried into the mineral realm via the etheric body. This substance, Steiner tells us, is deeply connected with the coagulation process. I can only assume that, as science becomes more able to detect activity of substances in very high dilution, it will be discovered that, at some crucial point or points within the vast ecology of blood biochemistry, antimony acts as a kind of catalyst. In homoeopathic medicine it has always been known that antimony can help in treating cases of excessive bleeding. It is only from Steiner's indications, however, that we know that this activity is connected to the deepest formative principles in the physical body, particularly the organization of the senses, in which matter altogether is precipitated from the realm of time and comes into spacial manifestation.

I also have the impression that antimony may be active at that interface between protein in the blood and protein within muscle. Seen imaginatively, muscle is, after all, very similar to coagulated blood. Antimony may play its part in this dynamic interplay, too. In any event, its main sphere of activity lies in between the etheric body and the physical body where it acts as a kind of mediator of the highest formative principles of the human being. Antimony was regarded as an almost universal remedy by Paracelsus, who I gather was also reputed to have said: "Antimony *Christus est.*" Steiner acknowledges that antimony has a very wide ranging and far reaching sphere of activity and perhaps it is even possible to imagine a relationship between antimony and the restoration of the archetype of the human form by Christ on Golgotha, working once more in this boundary region between time and space. This opens up the subject of the human phantom and its deepest relation to the resurrection body, and to its formative future tasks.

What is described in Steiner's lecture "The Etherization of the Blood" are really the counter processes to those which are described in the lecture "The Work of the Angels in the Astral Body." In the latter we have the picture of the degenerated processes that may arise in so far as the human being is not able to work consciously with his karma. To put it now in my own words, in "The Etherization of the Blood" the picture is presented of how, for the first time since the Mystery of Golgotha, it actually becomes possible for human beings to work with karma in such a way that a moral intention can be transformed into an effective deed in the same earthly life.

The lecture begins, you could almost say pessimistically, by first drawing attention to the polarity between the conscious life of thought and the unconscious life of will, connecting the former condition to waking consciousness and the latter to sleeping. Steiner goes on to say that true moral action can only come to expression through communing with our higher being in sleep and after death. One may sense a kind of implicit indication that the only hope for the wakeful human being is to keep open the back door to the spiritual world by sleep and death, but not to expect too much during this life. Steiner quickly moves on to point out that this was the situation that prevailed in the old mysteries before Golgotha. A new potential for humankind has now been established. Since Christ has entered earthly substance, the realm of matter, the radically new situation which arises through this deed confers on humankind the potential to become morally free and creative in waking day consciousness as well. The realm of dead matter has been united once again with the realm of creative moral action. In this sense, we may understand the phrase that Christ has, since the Mystery of Golgotha, become the Lord of Karma. And what does it mean to be a morally creative, free individual but to be able to begin to unfold love! This possibility was physiologically, biologically in danger of being lost before Golgotha, through the power of egoism combined with degeneration and hardening of our physical bodies. The realm of matter was taking hold of even humanity's good deeds and fixing them, distorting them, binding them to space — and ultimately even these would have been turned to evil effect.

One might say that matter and space were in danger of becoming both disembodied and decontextualized. At this very moment, as I am now speaking to you, and as you are hearing me, we have a contact from mouth to ear. This, of course, belongs to a particular moment in time, but having been once experienced it also belongs to eternity, because we are always able, at least potentially, and through exerting our will a little, to recreate this moment in our active memory, at least as long as we are healthy. It also lives on, of course, in the Akashic Records. But even an initiate can only re-enter this sphere through exerting considerable inner will.

If my lecture is recorded, printed and bound, however, fettered to the realm of space, it becomes decontextualized and disembodied. It may still be of help to the person who experienced it as a kind of *aide mémoire*, but to the person who reads it for the first time, in this form, it will not convey anything like the same experience as it carried in the moment of its happening. It falls out of action, that is to say, it passes from the realm of the "in-act" to the realm of the "ex-act." I like to imagine that "in-act" means intact, whole, in touch, integrated; "ex-act" means quantifiable, measurable, analytical.

This degeneration of the word, however, may be overcome in so far as we can now, through our own freedom, work into the world of space with new forces of will, trust and confidence in the future. When we do this, we are working with that physiological process within the blood which Steiner likens to etherization. In this lecture he describes how a stream is created which rises from the heart to that part of the brain connected with the pineal and pituitary glands. He says that a clairvoyant person is able to see, in the way a person wakes up or goes to sleep, the degree of a person's moral development by the way in which light interplays around his pituitary and pineal glands at that time. Morality is once again connected to the sleeping/waking polarity, but it is now possible to midwife a moral deed in waking day consciousness. This stream of etherization is at work in each of us since Golgotha, but it can only be turned into moral effect through a conscious recognition and understanding of the nature of Christ's Deed on earth. It is humanity's task from the present time and onwards into the future, to co-operate more and more with this stream, which is of course the same stream which works with the element of warmth when we generate an inner enthusiasm for the spirit, and which is outlined in Steiner's lectures entitled "The Bridge between Universal Spirituality and the Physical Consultation of Man." This will counteract the natural tendency of humankind to fall ever more and more strongly into degenerative illnesses of the immune system.

This moral process stands and falls on the possibility to find and work with one's karma. But to find one's karma means to find and connect oneself to those fellow human beings with whom one has to work and co-operate. This path cannot be trodden alone, because one cannot, by definition, find and work with one's karma on one's own — one can only accomplish this in the arena of our relationships which is, at one and the same time, an arena both of love and of pain. Finding and working with karma is, in the first instance, often painful. The birth pangs of discovering karma include the nightmares of painful relationships and as long as one carefully avoids one's karma one may go through life with apparently very easy relationships. Pain avoidance is one of the greatest threats in our time and it is synonymous with karma avoidance. It stands behind a great deal of so-called psychopathic behaviour and even much mental illness of the present day. Pain avoidance and the avoidance of suffering are to be equated with the avoidance of relationships and of karma.

Here we enter very clearly into the question which Parsifal asked to Amfortas, which, when rightly translated, means: "Brother, what confuses you?" It is confusion that is entering into human karma and it is the true task of healing to work with and overcome that confusion. Parsifal had been trained not to ask the painful question because pre-Christian initiation could not yet be inclusive of karma. Parsifal had to learn to blaze the trail of "karma inclusivity." In so far as there are indications to suggest that this being of Parsifal is connected to the being of Mani and the Manichean stream (see Lievegoed's *The Battle of the Soul*), we can sense that a preparation was taking place during this Grail incarnation for something which will only come to fruition in future times. A new kind of Christianity, one connected with identifying with the other, must gradually evolve. Love must rise from the realm of Eros into the realm of Agape, that is to say, into the possibility to identify with and carry the destiny of one's sister and brother. The seeds of the Manichean stream are to be found in the Grail saga and are intimately connected with the restoration of karma from confusion. This, in turn, is one and the same as the restoration of the integrity of the blood. The blood that cannot clot is lacking in those very formative forces which were reinstated in the material realm through Golgotha, and which enable the New Mysteries to be "karma-inclusive."

What does the image of the Holy Grail really signify? It is a kind of archetypal chalice or vessel which gives form to substance. Between the blood and the actual vessel there also lies the mystery between time and space, between the fluid and the solid, between coagulation and dispersion. One can add to these polarities those of sleeping and waking, of light and darkness. Held invisibly in the dynamic inner relationship between the blood and the vessel, there lies, in the deepest sense, the mystery of the rainbow, the mystery of that which links the realm of light and darkness and which was given by the Father God to humankind as an image of his healing Covenant. The Covenant was a kind of prophecy that in times to come it would once again be possible for the wakeful astral body to unite with up-building and not only destructive forces within the human organism. Our conscious astral body is dependent on catabolic or breakdown processes taking place in the physical body. But it may now also be raised through moral enthusiasm into that new stream that builds new substance for the future and in which consciousness once again becomes united with the hitherto unconscious forces of restoration.

To begin with, this rainbow could only be seen out there in the sky, as it were, as a token or image, or pointer of something to come — as a kind of covenant between fallen humankind and a future creative human potentiality. The covenant first needed the entry of the Christ Being into bone and into blood in order to become fact, and within our blood we have, in the most simple way, the spectrum of colours between the red in the arterial blood and the blue in the venous blood. But that which connects the two, the rainbow of radiant light which is the true light in the Grail, that is at a bodily level, invisible. We see the two poles with our earthly eyes but not that which inwardly unites them.

Those of you who have read D.H. Lawrence's novel *The Rainbow* may share my feeling that he, too, had a true sense for this future potentiality.

Into this red arterial blood — so says Rudolf Steiner — that which we taken in through our senses, dies. And in the periphery, between the lymphatic fluid and the venous blood, an impulse to movement is born which comes towards the centre from the periphery — this is the origin of the true movement or circulation of the blood. At that point where the venous blood gains its first impetus to return to the heart, new karma is born. With this a new light-source is generated which flows from the periphery to the centre, hidden in the darkness of the venous blood, creating new karmic possibilities to the future. This happens with every true act of free will. The mystery of the polarity between the arterial and venous blood encompasses the mystery of birth and death, of past and future, linked together as they are in time by the movement of the circulation. This "movement organism" also lives and resides between the polarity of heart and capillary. That which gives the original impulse to the movement becomes united, since the Mystery of Golgotha, with our inner possibility to be morally creative within our will, through the fact that the warmth process within our ether body becomes a light-engendering process too.

This is, I believe, the way in which Steiner is guiding us into a new understanding of human physiology, as nothing less than a manifestation of the highest spiritual task of humankind. It is also embodied and described in a hidden way in the Grail saga, and has to do with this new possibility of awakening creatively towards each other and placing our mutual karma in the service of a higher purpose, a higher task. This signature will be more and more essential in our practices, therapeutic centres and communities as time goes on, if they also are not to degenerate but are to become true "sun spaces," where new karma is built. This awakening to each other is, I believe, the beginning of the Manichean task, awakening new light for the future, working between the realms of time and space; you might also say, it is a task of "rainbow building."

The Bleeding Wound of King Amfortas

Karal Jan Tusenius

In his *Parsifal* legend, Wolfram von Eschenbach gives a detailed description of the condition of the seriously wounded King Amfortas. A bleeding and infected wound, incurred during a duel, will not heal, and causes so much discomfort and suffering that the King repeatedly begs the knights attending him in the Grail Castle to put an end to his life. The knights, however, do not respond to this request for euthanasia and regularly show him the Grail. This vessel, which is said to hold the blood of Christ, contains such strong life forces that the mortally sick King, who only wants to die, is repeatedly led back again to earthly life. Thus is the King destined to hover between life and death for many years.

At the beginning of this century, Rudolf Steiner lifted a part of the veil which covers this intriguing story. Parsifal, as a representative of the new period of individualized consciousness, has to meet and come to terms with his own destiny. Having been brought up by his mother in isolation from the life of the world, the inquisitive young man goes forth and, through trial and error, undergoes a process of development which seems

Parzival and Amfortas. Miniature from a Heidelberg manuscript.

remarkably modern, and which eventually puts him in a position to redeem the King from his sufferings. When he inquires after the destiny of the King, his wound closes up and healing ensues.

Shortly after the outbreak of the First World War, Rudolf Steiner deals with the then very topical subject of injury,[1] through which light is shed on the problem of the sick King and Parsifal's influence on him. He describes how, through an injury, the organism becomes vulnerable to a searing destructive life process from outside, from which it normally remains closed off. This pathological life process in turn attracts foreign life, such as bacteria, viruses and moulds. This probably points to a change in the etheric substance of the wounded or sick person. As a reaction to this disease process, the increased activity of the leucocytes, the white blood corpuscles, is described as the expression of a process of self consciousness, that is, an ego activity. These leucocytes which at the present time are still fulfilling their task in secret, are then described as the seeds of future consciousness. Furthermore, in this lecture reference is made to the fact that a helper can have a healing effect merely through his insight into, and consciousness of leucocyte activity.

The blood, "this hot, temperate, red humour, whose office is to nourish the whole body, to give it strength and colour, being dispersed in the veins through every part of it," as Robert Burton characterized it in 1628, thus appears to be playing a central role in the reaction to an injury. Can we recreate this picture by means of our present-day insight into the composition of the blood and the different regulatory mechanisms within it?

Substance and process in the blood

As the largest and least formed organ of the body, the blood is *par excellence* the bearer of the field of tension between physical substance and the working of processes. Once outside the body, the blood almost immediately degenerates into dead matter, while in the body it is able to perform its specific functions exclusively in a highly refined, dispersing and immaterial condition.

The blood passes through the body in a lemniscatory movement in which the so-called minor circulation involving the lungs alternates with the major circulation involving the rest of the body. In the heart the two blood streams cross. In the large, afferent (vein-like) and efferent (artery-like) blood vessels and in the atria and ventricles of the heart, the blood is visible in its "substantial" form; in these areas the blood is predominantly under the influence of physical laws. In the periphery, where the blood flows through capillaries, and to a certain extent leaves even these smallest of blood vessels, the blood is much less substantial and not, or hardly, subject to gravity. Thus there arises in these areas the possibility for the activity of non-physical influences. The rhythmic alteration between concentrating and diluting, between major and minor circulation, between the large vessels, the heart and the periphery, thus represents the interaction between the congesting and the sucking activities of the heart and the peripheral tissues. In this the heart plays a sensing (nerve-sense) and an impelling (metabolic) role.

Threefoldness of blood components

Might we be able to recognize the same threefoldness — the polarity between the formed and cool nerve-sense system and the unformed warm metabolic system, mediated by the mobile rhythmic system — so characteristic of the human being, in the components of the blood and their functions? The blood is a suspension of cells in plasma, a solution of protein and salts. The principal component of the blood plasma is water containing dissolved ions and three classes of proteins; carrier proteins, coagulation proteins and immunoproteins. The blood cells consist of red blood cells, (erythrocytes), platelets and white blood cells (leukocytes).

The main function of the red blood cells is to carry oxygen to the tissues and to return to the lungs carrying carbon dioxide.

Platelets work with the coagulation proteins to defend the circulatory system in the event of laceration or rupture.

The normal function of the white blood cells is to defend the organism against infection. So both in the plasma proteins and in the blood cells there is an interesting tripartite division consisting of, first: carrier proteins and carrying, hardly vital, red blood cells representing the *sal* principle. Second: coagulation proteins working together with the half-vital platelets in the field of maintaining a balance between structuring and dissolving processes, representing the *mercury* principle. And finally: immunoproteins and vital white blood cells, being the most autonomous and active part of the blood in the defence mechanisms, representing the *sulphur* principle. Already by encompassing the fluid and cellular divisions of the blood in one picture, a basic polarity is suggested within this largest organ of the human being. As we shall see, this polarity can be observed in almost every aspect of the blood.

Bleeding and clotting tendencies

In one of his lecture courses to doctors, Rudolf Steiner describes the relationship, within the blood, between forces from outside leading to clotting and the activity of the human ego which enhances the fluidity of the blood.[2] He calls the forces from outside the antimonizing forces (after the strongly structured metal antimony); the body's own dissolving power he describes as albuminizing after the Latin word *albumen*, representing the unformed, vitalizing element. In this lecture he connects the albuminizing principle with the substance-creating process and the conscious will, while the antimonizing principle is seen in relation to the way in which substances are ultimately formed and sculpted into organs.

Through the many influences from outside, the human being is at present strongly under the influence of the antimonizing forces.

The excessive clotting tendency of the blood on the one hand, and the increased tendency towards bleeding, on the other, are at present fairly well understood as far as the underlying mechanisms are concerned. The formation of a clot involves the gelling of a precursor protein, known as fibrinogen, into fibrin. This involves the sequence of reactions known as the clotting cascade, the effect of which is to amplify the tiny biochemical signal produced by a damaged vessel into a fibrin generating reaction vigorous enough to form a clot capable of stopping the bleeding from a damaged vessel. In other words, the clotting cascade is enhanced by an external injury such as already suggested by Rudolf Steiner over seventy years ago. As important as the formation of a clot at the site of injury is its removal when its usefulness is over. The clot is removed by enzymatic digestion, a process referred to as fibrinolysis. This is accomplished by enzymes from tissue cells, blood vessel cells and certain leucocytes. Here again we see a striking correspondence with Steiner's association of the dilution forces in the blood with the metabolic pole. Finally, Steiner's statement in this lecture about the future domination of the antimony process in the human being due to the increase in external influences, is impressively illustrated by the growing number of patients with sclerotic vessel diseases who need anticoagulation therapy to prevent spontaneous blood clotting.

The blood as an organ of defence

How can we come to a clearer understanding of the previously mentioned statement by Steiner regarding the leucocytes as bearers of consciousness?

Among the leucocytes a certain developmental specialization takes place. We distinguish between granulocytes, monocytes and macrophages and lymphocytes As we shall see later, these sub-divisions fulfil, respectively, executive, communication and decision-making functions within the "army" of leucocytes, which is called into action by invading micro-organisms.

In the last century a connection had already been made between infections and the appearance of bacteria on the one hand, and the various defence mechanisms of leucocytes against infections, on the other. It remained the subject of heated debate for many decades, whether this defence was the result of certain leucocytes which attacked and devoured the bacteria, as observed in starfish by the Russian physiologist Metchnikoff in 1882 or whether it was the result of substances circulating in the blood, as postulated by Pasteur and von Behring. Since the beginning of the century it has become clear that our immunity has cellular as well as humoural aspects and thus the arguments between the two schools of thought could be laid to rest.

What happens when a harmful intruder (antigen) manages to cross the natural barriers of skin or mucous membrane? When such an antigen reaches the blood circulation it will first of all encounter a number of macrophages, the inquisitors of the leucocyte army. A portion of these antigens will then be directly attacked by the macrophages (non-specific immunity) and swallowed up (phagocytosis). In this process the granulocytes (the infantry) too are often involved. A further proportion of the antigens become attached to the macrophages and are offered to higher members of the defence system, the lymphocytes (the officers of the leucocyte army — specific immunity), for identification. This highest echelon of defence is in turn divided into B-lymphocytes and various T-lymphocytes, which communicate with each other and with lower sub-divisions of the defensive apparatus after having come into contact with an antigen. In response to antigens presented to them by the macrophages, the B-lymphocytes produce antibodies: immunoglobulins, which attach themselves specifically to particular antigens and eventually lead to their destruction. In certain circumstances the T-lymphocytes can attack the antigens directly (cell mediated immunity), while in other cases they merely regulate the defence mechanism.

The T-helper and T-suppressor cells respectively stimulate or suppress the defensive response through influencing the antibody formation of the B-lymphocytes. The T-helper cells, the most important sub-division of the immune system, are the specific target of the AIDS virus. AIDS patients, in whom the number of T-helper cells is dramatically reduced, thus become vulnerable to all sorts of infections which usually lead to their death. This would not be able to happen in a normally functioning system of immunological defence.

The defence system of the human body can not only be weakened, but may also be overactive, leading to different kinds of illnesses. In cases of hypersensitivity (allergy), the wrong kind of antibodies is produced, often in vastly increased quantities. In all kinds of auto-immune diseases (among others, systemic lupus enthyematosis, rheumatoid arthritis, certain forms of diabetes mellitus, etc.) defensive cells are produced against healthy cells of the patient's own body. In summary, our defensive apparatus is very complex in structure, certain parts displaying more the metabolic dynamic (granulocytes), others more the dynamic of the nerve-sense system (T-lymphocytes). Its task is to distinguish the harmful outside world (antigens) from the body's own elements (identity) and, where necessary, to take specific or non-specific measures to eliminate these foreign elements (immunity). Thus the immune process seems to display to a high degree aspects of the preservation of identity and of personality, which is characteristic of ego function.

Blood formation as an expression of ego activity

At the beginning of the embryonic phase of development, the foetus's blood supply (symbolizing the individual ego) originates in the periphery. During the process of embryonic development, the blood forming process becomes more centralized as its production by the liver and spleen is taken over by the bone marrow — representing a process of ego internalization. The origin of blood within the bone marrow can of itself be seen as a polarity in which the most living and cosmic substance of the body is produced in the almost dead skeleton. Interestingly, in some diseases this process becomes reversed, indicating that the ego has lost its influence over the process, as is seen in leukaemia. In these cases the blood formation process is displaced from the bone marrow outward toward the liver, spleen or even skin — which represents a process of externalization.

In the previously mentioned lecture by Rudolf Steiner about injury, where leucocytes are described as representatives of forces of consciousness, ego functions are also pointed to. These are mobilized through invading, destructive, world ether forces entering the body through the wound. In modern immunological terminology the reaction of the etheric body against this invading bit of the outside world (antigen) is called antibody. This terminology very strongly characterizes the dynamic of the etheric body, which sets itself against the laws of the physical world.

Hygienic occultism

With this term Rudolf Steiner points to a capacity to be developed within medicine in the period of the consciousness soul, through which insight can be gained into the relationship between illness and biography, thus leading to the power to heal.[3] In short, Rudolf Steiner develops the concept that during an illness a person goes through his whole biography in a very concentrated form. This means that illness signifies far more than a disturbance from outside. Viewed in this light, illness has to do with the personal development of the individual, or with the elements of stagnation within it. To the extent that insight into the relationship between illness and biography is developed, one gains a grip on the illness, which is no longer regarded as an isolated or arbitrary phenomenon.

Let us now return to the introduction to this article, in which the mortally wounded King Amfortas was presented. Wolfram von Eschenbach describes how in his youth the King was struck by a poisoned lance. The resulting wound would not heal and remained in a state of putrid infection.

This conjures up the image of the destructive world ether which cannot be sufficiently overcome by the power of the leucocytes, representing consciousness. Chrétien de Troyes, in his *Parsifal* legend, describes the King's wound as the ever-bleeding tip of the lance. With reference to Rudolf Steiner's statement regarding the polarity between blood clotting and excessive bleeding, this could suggest that in the King's body there is a shortage of externally formative antimonizing consciousness soul forces.

Parsifal, who at his first meeting with the sick King, had not yet progressed far enough along his own path of development to be able to ask the redeeming question, has to go through a further five years of privations before he sees the King again. Then, by asking the question: "How has your destiny come into such disarray?" he is able to heal the King and become Grail King himself. Parsifal, as the first representative of the consciousness-soul human being, shows evidence of having developed the above-mentioned hygienic occult powers, together with the respective antimonizing therapeutic attitude. Through insight into the laws of destiny or karma, he has powers at his disposal by means of which he is able to transcend himself and his environment.

Translated from the Dutch by Carlotta Hollmann Dyson

References
1. R. Steiner, lecture of August 13, 1914 *(Samariterkurs,* Vol. 253 of the complete Works).
2. R. Steiner, *Spiritual Science and Medicine,* Chap. 19 (Vol. 312).
3. R. Steiner, "The Challenge of the Times," Lecture 3, December 1, 1918 (Vol. 186).

D.H. Lawrence's *The Rainbow*, the Lion and the Blood of Sophia

Andrew Welburn

Readers of modern literature find it hard to forget the almost pulsating directness of D.H. Lawrence's *The Rainbow* — above all in its opening chapter. It is less the sense of the landscape, though that is strongly evoked, with its marshy flatness and abruptly rising Ilkeston church-tower, and more the extraordinary manner of Lawrence's apprehending of it that strikes us. What he describes is hardly the Brangwen family's view of things, or of their life and social world, though those are mentioned, especially in their awed and "epic" impression of the wider life at Shelly Hall. It is something more deeply rooted, involved in their exhausting physical labour on the land, in their engagement with growth and reproduction of animals and the yearly surge of life in the fields. It hardly allows them space to step back and form a view of life, or even to set for themselves a goal:

> But heaven and earth was teeming around them, and how should this cease? They felt the rush of the sap in spring, they knew the wave which cannot halt, but every year throws forward the seed to begetting, and, falling back, leaves the young-born on the earth. They knew the intercourse between heaven and earth, sunshine drawn into the breast and bowels, the rain sucked up in the daytime, nakedness that comes under the wind in autumn, showing the birds' nests no longer worth hiding. Their life and interrelations were such; feeling the pulse and body of the soil, that opened to their furrow for the grain, and became smooth and supple after their ploughing, and clung to their feet with a weight that pulled like desire, lying hard and unresponsive when the crops were to be shorn away ...

The scarcely conscious and deeply significant slip of "was" with "heaven and earth" shows that there is no detachment in this apprehension of things, but a brimming fullness of involvement. Nothing comes to meet us from without, but is left stranded only by the wash of the tide that will inevitably return to refloat it, drawing us into the ebb and flow that will toss the next manifestation of life onto the shore. Life within meets living, pulsating life without:

> They took the udder of the cows, the cows yielded milk and pulse against the hands of the men, the pulse of the blood of the teats of the cows beat into the pulse of the hands of the

men. They mounted their horses, and held life between the grip of their knees, they harnessed their horses at the wagon, and, with hand on the bridle-rings, drew the heaving of the horses after their will.

This is the world apprehended, not in the mode of detachment that reflects the perspective of head-knowledge but through a perceptive power awakened, as it were, in the rhythmic system. The pounding and circulating of the blood has become a sort of organ of prehension, itself breathing, pulsing, heaving in the enjoyment of life.

Studies, such as the one by Frank Kermode, have shown that Lawrence was aware of esoteric teachings, and even of methods which have been used in esoteric training to develop faculties of higher perception. He would have sympathized with Steiner's conception of all the human organism, not just the nervous system, conveying the life of the soul and spirit. Certainly he knew about Theosophy, and also much of the lore of the Apocalypse in the writings of the twelfth-century mystical Abbot Joachim of Fiore, whose vision of the Three Ages, under the Father, Son and Holy Spirit, threw a vast span across history and provided the underpinning for the structure of *The Rainbow.* Its three generations which the novel traces seem to echo the rhythm of cosmic cycles in history itself. And it culminates in Ursula's rainbow-vision of the Age of the Spirit:

> She saw in the rainbow the earth's new architecture, the old, brittle corruption of houses and factories swept away, the world built up in a

living fabric of Truth, fitting to the over-arching heaven.

Lawrence never surpassed the achievement of this book, or convinced us more thoroughly of his perceptual powers.

Lawrence was committed to his "blood-philosophy" because it enabled him to understand much about human nature that the usual head-perspective falsified. Above all sexual life; and, related to that, community in general. The cultivation of head-consciousness had destroyed the kind of togetherness in experience that he had known in his childhood in the mining communities of the Midlands where he set *The Rainbow*. The model provided a diagnosis, indeed, for the ills of society at large. Rudolf Steiner also stressed the impossibility of conjuring social reality out of ideas, out of the head. That could produce only utopias and disappointments, nightmares of revolutionary idealism followed by destruction, cycles of oppression. In the revolution brewing in Russia, and the programmes that were being put forward for it in the first decade of the twentieth century, Steiner saw much that violated the principles of human nature. New social structures were expected to provide the panaceas long sought in vain, but were based on no clear understanding of what brings people together, or what gives them a sense of collective effort and identity of will. The head, in Steiner's terms, is cosmically old. He sought in new and striking ways to rediscover the "forces of rejuvenation": and that meant understanding the perceptions of the rhythmic system. It meant understanding the things which had been conveyed imaginatively in ancient myths, and the societies which lived by them. It was not, as Lawrence rather suggested, that we could never get beyond our rootedness in blood-ties and forms of life that were tied to the land, or relationships that expressed the bonds of sex and of origins. That was precisely Steiner's point: whilst those things ran rhythmically on, in traditional cultures and even in much of pre-Industrial modern Europe, there was neither the need nor the possibility of understanding them; it was in order to grasp the forces of change, to bring people together in new ways, that we needed to be able to understand the powers beating in the blood, and tirelessly renewing our life through the air we breathe.

In previous times, such things had been a matter for the Mysteries. Ordinary people did not have the highly developed sense of self which can direct processes of change: it was the initiated leaders and priests who shaped society. the Apocalypse itself is the ultimate vision of change, of a new heaven, earth and a "heavenly Jerusalem" descending onto the earth. Lawrence's simple opposition between the head-consciousness and the heart's blood has therefore to be complicated by a vision of a balance and interaction of forces in the modern world, when what was once only for the chosen is increasingly required and demanded by the struggling individual. Lawrence's rejection of the head, in fact, opened the way for all kinds of atavistic elements which, especially in later novels like *The Plumed Serpent*, suggest that the individual is liable to be suppressed by the cult of the powerful will. A new Mystery cult is indeed created, but it is the Mexican Mysteries that Lawrence looks to in his desperation to find a force powerful enough to ram through the changes he no longer trusts people to want or share in creating. Links between his "blood-philosophy" and the Fascist movements which based themselves on distortedly similar ideas are not hard to detect. But in the Mysteries of ancient times which helped to shape the great cultural achievements of classical drama and in the Mysteries which Rudolf Steiner sought to make the basis of a new social and cultural life, understanding the potent spirituality inherent in the blood means precisely a grasp of its role in human nature as a whole — a human wisdom, or anthroposophy.

The contrast comes home, perhaps, in reading Lawrence's strange and unbalanced, if profound little book simply called *Apocalypse*. Too personal to be called a Commentary, it embodies a response to the imaginative energy of the Apocalypse that is unrivalled by any theologian. It shows at the same time, however, the inability of the natural man to comprehend the reorientation of the faculties that initiation necessarily brings about. Steiner characterized the change of perspective which underlies the apocalyptist's visions; Lawrence still supposes that they express only the head-perspective and its fear of the dynamic, rhythmic nature.

Dangers there certainly are on this path to the awakening of deeper faculties of perception. Lawrence's own imbalance and twentieth-century history, including the nightmare of Nazism, leave that in no doubt. But the Apocalypse does not quail before them. Rather it shows us a way, in its esoteric mythologies, in which the blood-forces can be harnessed for the future good of humanity, if we can learn to open its seals. For history is the book with seven seals which the seer is shown in heaven. And the opening of it is achieved only with the appearance of a significant figure: the Lion of Judah. This Lion shares in the riddling quality of the other apocalyptic symbols, and in fact we can never fully appreciate its meaning unless we are able, as was Rudolf Steiner, to recognize in it an imagination that belongs to a certain stage on the path of transformation. Steiner entered into this imagination in a lecture given during the First World War, in which he describes the deepening of consciousness and the processes connected with it, and in particular the forces awakened in the rhythmic system. A balance of inner powers is already required as soon as we take the step from the head-consciousness into the domain of elemental forces that we now encounter. The quest for that balance becomes a struggle with the Lion.

The context is always an historical one. The rhythmic life of humanity can never be considered just subjectively: it is the realm of sharing, of doing things together or participating in a common destiny. The power of actively controlling our thoughts, through knowledge of the forces lying behind and producing them, Steiner therefore explains, is only to be gained through an ability to identify with our destiny. Normally we tend to suppose that thoughts are shaped just by our own inner processes. But our approach to working creatively with the powers of thought must be a circuitous one. It is achieved, he points out, only gradually; but slowly "our thoughts assume a character identical with our own essential character." However, the will power that we need "now presents itself before us as a fearsome beast":

> In the mystical tradition this has for thousands of years been known as "meeting the lion." This

> encounter with the lion has to be gone through. It consists in a feeling of abject terror concerning what has to be done in the thought-world, great fear of entering into a living union with the thought-world. This terror must be overcome. Just as the sense of isolation has to be overcome at the "Gate of Death" stage. We feel terror: this terror may present itself in all kinds of ways ...

Certainly many of Lawrence's characters struggle with these inner terrors in their search for a way beyond the alienation of head-bound thinking he longed to replace. Perhaps, too, many people felt them in the earlier part of this century as an inability to identify with their destiny — an inability to move history on. And as a result, they were given up to the dark side of the forces circulating in their blood. For Steiner continues by explaining how we attain to a higher development of consciousness only by drawing on certain concealed resources. We have to find the way, he insists, of fitting in with the harmonies of the realm into which we are entering, when we leave behind the sort of awareness that is limited to the body.

> We must fit into the cosmic harmonies. And the forces to be used out there are also within us: it is only that they function at an unconscious level — the forces that make the blood move, make our hearts beat, derive from spiritual entities. And we become immersed in these when we immerse ourselves in the element of will. These forces are within us. If someone is taken hold of

> by the element of will without having followed the regular esoteric path, he is taken hold of by the forces that normally circulate in his blood, beat in his heart. He is then not using the forces that exist outside the body, but forces present within his body ...

Millions of people were indeed obsessed by these will-forces, the forces of unconscious life beating in the blood. The result was a ghastly parody of Christian apocalypse: a retardation of history, the spreading of terror, the annihilation of humanity.

That is why it is so important, on the esoteric path, continues Steiner, that we have the "meeting with the lion." It is a staggering experience which helps to bring about the inner reorientation of perspectives:

> The Imagination paints a very vivid picture of the beast opening its huge jaws ready to devour us. The will-power we want to use in the spiritual world is threatening to devour us. All the time the overriding sensation is that we must use our will, we must do something, we need to take hold of one thing or another, and at the same time another feeling arises in connection with all these elements of will activity into which we are entering. It is the feeling that they will devour us if we take hold of them, extinguish us in the world. That is the lion devouring us. What we must literally do — to stay with the metaphor — is not to give in to fears that the will elements may take hold of us there in the spiritual world, devour us and strangle us; no, we must mount

> the lion and take hold of those will elements, using them to effect our deeds.

We must master the lion or it will master us: that is the heart of the matter.

I have quoted Steiner's illuminating description at length, because so far as I know there was, when he spoke, no other account of this Imagination — which he nevertheless asserts was well known for some "thousands of years." The situation changed only after 1945. Something of the mystery behind the figure of the apocalyptic lion, who opens the seals and moves history forward in spiritual significance, was rediscovered. The accidental uncovering of early Christian and especially Christian-Gnostic texts by peasants in Upper Egypt, at the tiny village of Nag Hammadi, restored to the world the *Gospel of Thomas*.

Although it took the world some time to realize it, the Nag Hammadi discovery had brought it a document containing a very early, and very authentic tradition of the teachings of Jesus. The *Gospel of Thomas* consists almost entirely of sayings of Jesus, with very little indication of situation, still less of narrative or event. That was assumed, perhaps, since the teachings were still at a highly esoteric stage: these are "secret sayings," handed on by the apostles to those found worthy to receive them. Gradually, the sayings came to be written down. Gradually, again, the simple form of collected "sayings of the Lord" evolved into fuller presentations of the life of Jesus — the familiar type of gospel we know from the New Testament. From the beginning, however, the sayings or the life were not mere reminiscences: they formed a path of spiritual development through the deeper dimension that gave meaning to the words or to the context in which they were given. "Whoever finds the interpretation of these sayings will not experience death" is the very first in the whole collection of the *Gospel of Thomas*. The Gospel indeed constitutes new evidence for Rudolf Steiner's view that Christianity in its origins had close links with the Mysteries, the initiation-centres of the ancient world. The most interesting theory is that of G. Quispel, who has pointed to several signs of use of the Gospel by the Hermetic Mysteries, which had their origin and centre in Egypt, but also had branches in Syria, where the *Gospel of Thomas* came to be written down.

Among the enigmatic sayings which have puzzled scholars is one about a lion:

> Jesus said: Blessed is the lion which a man consumes, and the lion becomes man; and cursed is the man whom the lion consumes, and the lion becomes man. *(Gospel of Thomas 7)*

So strange did the picture of a lion-eating man appear, and so unusual the repeated notion of the lion becoming man, that some scholars have sought to reconstruct the text in other ways. But Rudolf Steiner has given us a clear understanding of what is involved in the spiritual stage to which the Saying refers. Both halves of the Saying concern the way in which the forces of blood-circulation, which carry consciousness into the great world, the macrocosm, "become man," that is, are actualized in the spiritual development of a person who has reached the stage of the "meeting with the lion." That may happen, as Steiner pointed out, in a positive way —

but it may also lead, if the preparation has been inadequate, to the unleashing of forces which the individual cannot control, the will-forces of our own bodily nature. So the release of the blood-forces can be either a blessing or a curse, as is the case with all spiritual development, depending entirely upon the way it is undertaken and integrated into our mode of life and level of maturity. If the fear overtakes us, the lion will indeed open its jaws and swallow us, consume as and become man by taking us over. By a further extension of the metaphor, however, the *Gospel of Thomas* speaks of the reverse possibility as the man consuming — devouring and assimilating to himself — the lion. That is the "blessed" way in which "the lion becomes man," according to this fragment of the Mystery-teaching of Jesus, which is brilliantly illuminated by the quite independent spiritual teachings of Rudolf Steiner some thirty years prior to the Gospel's discovery in the cliffs by the Nile.

The relevance of some, at least, among these rediscovered fragments of esoteric teaching to our modern age should already be obvious. The *Gospel of Thomas* too connects such experiences with apocalyptic change — the transition to new ages, when humanity presumably is expected to have new faculties. But it constantly focuses the moving power of transition in individuals, in those who can unfold the faculties in a "blessed" manner. Several times it adds explicitly, "and they shall not fear." It is one of the tragedies of world-history that the Church did not succeed in keeping in touch with its esoteric origins. Though it preserved the Gospels, and even the Apocalypse, which are based on esoteric insights, it failed to keep alive the techniques by which individuals could arrive at spiritual perception, through the "meeting with the lion," through the death-and-resurrection of initiation. It preserved the ideas behind them only as beliefs. The extraordinary contents of the Nag Hammadi library show us, on the other hand, that outside the increasingly institutionalized Church, small groups of Gnostics carried on the initiation methods, both in their archaic, Mystery form and even, to some extent, in their Christian form, with a relationship to the historical figure, however it may have been conceived, of Jesus.

Another Nag Hammadi work, *On the Origin of the World*, takes us into the cosmic dimension of Gnostic mythology. It belongs, certainly, to the line of Gnostic thought which had cut its ties with historical Christianity. Yet it is clearly grounded in the same mystical experience of "meeting the lion." It now demands, however, that we be willing to leap to that cosmic perspective which the ordinary, head-orientated self finds threatening and fearful. In fact, its startling narrative only makes sense when we realize that once again we are in the domain of the rhythmic blood-forces, treated now as cosmic formative forces in a sort of embryology. The blood-circulation is the vehicle for shaping, cosmic forces which actually underlie the genesis of the human form. In the myth about the divine Sophia, and the catastrophic events which bring into being the material world and the human body out of the spiritual, we recognize the same themes of creativity and danger, of blood and the lion, of a possible transformation of consciousness.

The "lion" again meets us as a powerful and threatening being, termed here an "archon," that is, a cosmic power. On one level it dramatizes the effect that possession by the darker possibilities of the blood-forces would have. It is arrogant, full of a sense of power, yet darkened and self-enclosed:

> When the archon saw his greatness — and he saw only himself; he saw nothing else except water and darkness — then he thought that he alone existed. His thought was made complete by his word, and it appeared as a spirit moving to and fro over the waters ...

Its material energy and greatness develop into a parody of the Creator God. In fact we know from parallel versions of the myth that the archon's word was a blasphemous "I am God, and apart from me there is no other" — for which he is instantly rebuked by the higher worlds. But behind this, as we know from Rudolf Steiner, stands the real parallel between the processes of embryonic formation in the womb and the cosmic events of the creation, of the emergence of the universe in spiritual evolution. The archon is in one sense a half-formed, lion-like foetus in the watery darkness of the womb — perhaps that is why some accounts say that he is something between a serpent and a lion, recalling the strange early stages of human development — and in another he does indeed contain vast cosmic forces of creation, still working in the rhythmic system and the beating blood, even though in the head-system they have long since produced their finished product with its characteristic detachment.

The myth is obviously showing us, therefore, the dangers of the lion-power; but it reveals at the same time that its powers are those of cosmic creativity, and of

THE RAINBOW, THE LION AND THE BLOOD OF SOPHIA   69

our own formation out of the cosmos. Unless we learn how to harness those forces rightly, the result will be not a birth but an abortion — which is how the archon is described, and how it would be if the lion were born and "became a man" at this imperfect stage. The rest of the Gnostic myth fills in the context, and it should now I think be intelligible as an account of inner processes and the Imaginations which accompany them. For it tells how, prior to the material creation, Sophia existed as a feminine emanation of God. But she tried to create something without being in harmony with her "partner," her corresponding power in the higher regions. As a result she herself was riven by terrible sufferings, and the raw material of matter, chaotic and dark, originated from her. The text *On the Origin of the World* describes it in vivid biological detail:

> Just as all the useless afterbirth of one who bears a little child fails, likewise the matter which came into being ... the matter of Chaos which was cast off like a miscarriage since there was no spirit in her. For all of that is a boundless darkness and water of unfathomable depth. And when Pistis (Sophia) saw what came into being from her deficiency she was disturbed. And the disturbance appeared as a fearful work ... an archon which appeared out of the waters, lion-like in appearance, male-female, and having a great authority within him, but not knowing whence he came into being.

From a later passage in the text it seems that menstruation is interpreted as a reminder of this process — and we know from other sources that the Gnostics regarded menstrual blood and other secretions as vehicles of spiritual powers. But it is clear overall that the myth tells us of exactly the process which Steiner explained. It tells of how we come to be in the power of the fearful lion. And the forces active in us, such as Sophia, rightly figure as primordial powers of creation, which brought the world as we know it into existence. The events of our inner life are being characterized from the cosmic dimension, of which they are an echo in our finite forms.

Once we understand this, we will also understand why the Gnostic creation-myth demands a complementary apocalyptic vision such as appears at the end of *On the Origin of the World*. For the logic of the myth, and of its inner meaning, demands that we be shown in addition the fulfilment of these forces when Sophia is brought into harmony with the higher powers, that is, when we follow the proper path of initiatory development. And in all versions of the myth, the higher power who comes to fulfil the role of Sophia's "partner" is — the Christ.

Like the disturbing symbols of the Apocalypse, the Gnostic myths can seem frightening and obscure until we attain to that reorientation of consciousness which allows us to interpret them. But, for the lack of such teachings, attempts like those of powerful imaginations such as D.H. Lawrence to open up a deeper dimension of living awareness have been unable to escape the dangers which attend upon them. With the help of those with spiritual insight from esoteric knowledge, such as Rudolf Steiner, however, it is still possible to see how the overcoming of the fearful threat of the lion must inevitably lead to the opening of the apocalyptic seal in a healthy and evolutionary way, which is to say that consciousness advances to an awareness of the rhythmic life-sphere. The Lion of Judah will indeed open the seal of history. For the vision of the threatening lion is a step on the way to the vision of that higher power with whom Sophia can put us in harmony. The fulfilment of the vision for which the twentieth century is striving is that of Christ in the sphere of living, etheric forces. Aware of the dangers attendant on our mistakes, it is for us to continue the quest for that vision with all our hearts.

Mithras, the Bull, and the Transformation of the Blood

Christopher Clouder

"You've been saved by the shedding of blood that makes you immortal!" Such were the words spoken by a priest of Mithras after the rite of the Taurobolium. In this ritual the aspirant had entered the temple of Mithras, taken his leave of all assembled there and climbed down into a pit that was in front of the altar, which was then covered with a wooden lattice. A bull was led in, placed on the grid and then ceremoniously slaughtered. The blood of the sacrificial animal would then have poured down into the pit and drenched the votary below, he would even be expected to moisten his tongue with it. After emerging from this baptism of blood he would be hailed as someone who had "been reborn forever." This has parallels in the *Nibelungenlied* where Siegfried, having been bathed in the blood of the dragon he had beaten in combat, found he could consequently understand the language of the birds. He had reached a stage of higher consciousness.

The ritual would have taken place in a subterranean vault, or "cave," lit only by oil lamps. These Mithraic centres were small, only accommodating a limited number of people. On the altar itself there was often a sculptured representation of the original Taurobolium where Mithras himself, wearing his Phrygian cap of initiation, would be depicted plunging his iron sword into the neck of a bull. This is the bull that had been created by Ahuro Mazdao and miraculously tamed by Mithras, but needed to be slain to preserve it from falling into the realm of Ahriman. Mithras had been born in a cave on the 25th of December and venerated by shepherds as the *Sol Invictus,* the unconquerable sun. For his followers Sunday was a holy day, most of the initiation rites took place around the Easter season and they addressed each other as "brother" and the priest as "father," as did the early Christians. Although it was exclusively a male religion, the female worshippers of the Phrygian goddess Cybele, the great mother, had a very similar ritual.

According to St Augustine, the priests of Mithras were in the habit of saying: "That one in the cap (that is, Mithras) is a Christian, too," and in spite of our modern sensibilities regarding their rites, we must recognize that they were striving for a high moral order. A Persian Mithraic text states: "He who will not eat of my body and drink of my blood, so that he will be made with one with me and I with him, the same shall not know salvation." In the marble statue of the deed of Mithras, now in the British Museum, the blood pouring from the sacrifice actually turns into three ears of wheat. Rudolf Steiner describes animal sacrifice as an attempt to raise old clairvoyant powers that had already diminished by the third post-Atlantean epoch when the Magi in

Mithras slaying the bull. British Museum.

Babylon turned the veneration of Mithras into a secret sect. They felt that because the god of light was no longer visible for humanity, a special training was necessary to anticipate his glorious manifestation as Mithras, the great sun king. Through this a deeper insight could be gained into the working of the universe. Although by the time of Augustus a certain decadence had crept in, the effect was still, however, the attainment of a certain self knowledge through the physical organism which was achieved by a "sudden contradiction of the astral and etheric bodies."

For the Mithraist the universe was in a state of perpetual battle between what was intrinsically good and evil. Mithras, as a lower god, had been sent to assist the good and participate in the redeeming of the cosmos. This battle was continued after death when angels and devils would struggle for the possession of souls. Earthly life was a mirror of the cosmic. Inwardly the believer was expected to make his life a continual reenactment of the created bull sacrifice. This tenet spread rapidly through the Roman army giving a deeper meaning to their professional activities, and where there was a ready parallel of a soldier rising through the ranks and the various grades of initiation. One had to mortify the purely physical and then the life-giving spirit could flow which would "transform what you had absorbed on the way down and carry it upward to the spiritual world." The blood in which one bathed as a warrior of Mithras was permeated with the warmth of the sun and through this act Mithras could unite with one's own striving:

> The priests of Mithras went on to say, "Man must therefore battle against the bull nature — the

animal nature — within him with the help of something which is higher. He must conquer the nature that gives him this lower form of wisdom. ... When we make man aware of the sun forces within him, he himself is Mithras, the conqueror of the bull." This was the image presented in the cult. It was not an invented symbol; its purpose was to present the relevant cosmological truth. The religious rite was far more than an external symbol; it was something that had been drawn as it were out of the very essence of the universe."[1]

Blood, and its substitute red ochre, has been used since prehistoric times as part of the rituals associated with rites of passage. Red ochre, ferric oxide, is constituted from iron and oxygen and there is no evidence of it being in existence before the arrival of oxygen-producing algae. As a mineral, therefore, it is intimately connected with life and is an exterior form of our own blood. Early humanity had a strong sense of this interpenetration of our outer environment and our inner organic life. Red ochre was collected and kept in the Terra Amata Cave, near Nice, three hundred and fifty thousand years ago. Many Neanderthal skeletons have been found curled up in a foetus position as though asleep and then sprinkled with this red pigment both in Africa and the Middle East. In the Aurignacian period around 30,000 BC this sprinkling of red ochre on the dead spread into western Europe and reached as far as Siberia. In some sites of human dwellings the earth is impregnated with this colour to a depth of twenty centimetres. This all suggests it was used more than for its medicinal properties as an antiseptic.

Red ochre is also the main pigment found in cave paintings of the Paleolithic times. Later uses are to be found such as in the covering of the tabernacle of the Israelites with skins dyed red and the Israelites also used the ashes of a red heifer for purifying the hands of those who had come into contact with death. "Tell the people of Israel to bring you a red heifer without defect, in which there is no blemish, and upon which a yoke has never been placed." (Numbers 19.2) It has been claimed that the sphinx was painted red. Its use continues to this day in marriage ceremonies in modern India and it is the colour that distinguishes the Roman pontiff and the cardinals.

With its connection with oxygenization the rituals of the blood were like the experience of inhalation. The experiences for the aspirant going through such trials were akin to those of in-breathing. The initiation of exhalation was of the nature practised by John the Baptist:

> Externally, of course, John the Baptist baptized with the waters of Jordan. We know that the candidates for baptism suffered total immersion. During the immersion they experienced a kind of loosening of the etheric body, which bestowed on them a temporary clairvoyance. What was the purpose of the baptism with water in the Jordan? It was intended that through the loosening of their etheric bodies and experiences they underwent, the candidates for baptism should feel themselves transposed into the condition of consciousness of the time before the Fall. Everything which had occurred

since the Fall was to be erased from their consciousness.[2]

Both these forms of purification are related to the old Persian festivals of fire and water and are an attempt to revive an earlier form of consciousness, in fact baptism of remembrance. However, we can see in both parallels with the early Christians and their beliefs. In the catacombs the predominant colour for the wall paintings was again red ochre and their themes were those of transformation and rebirth. Like the worshippers of Mithras and the cave dwellers of Paleolithic times, we are again in the company of the dead but in a very different context:

> Mithraism was regarded as a genuine form of worship connected with the sun forces in man. Only in this Mithraic worship it was not yet realized that in preparation for the Mystery of Golgotha the sun force itself had descended as a spiritual being and united with the man, Jesus of Nazareth. *(Aspects of Ancient Wisdom)*

There are very few portrayals of the Crucifixion in the first centuries after Christ and wherever it is to be found it is to emphasize the deed of resurrection and universal solution through the Cross. It is not until the beginning of the Middle Ages that the subject of the Crucifixion was used as representing the death of Jesus and the blood shown coming from the wounds and trickling down to penetrate the earth. A fundamental change of consciousness had occurred. Before the Mystery of Golgotha:

people believed the deity works through the blood and through the body. This led them to believe that when the blood flows through the veins of the human being or the animals, it is really taken away from the gods. It is the rightful possession of the gods. Therefore, human beings can approach the gods if they return blood to them. The gods really wish to keep the blood to themselves; humans have taken possession of it. In turn, human beings must give the blood back to the gods, hence the blood sacrifice of the ancient times.

Then came the teachings of Christ:

> Look upon what works in the human being prior to the earth's influence on him: take bread, something that nourishes human beings, and look at how they initially partake of it. They partake of it by means of a sense of taste. The food in human beings goes to a certain point before it is transformed into blood. For it is only changed into blood after having passed through the walls of the intestines into the organism. Only there does the earth's influence begin; as long as the food has not been taken hold of by the blood, the earth's influence has not yet begun. Therefore, do not view blood as something corresponding to the god; behold that in the bread before it turns into blood and in the wine before it enters the blood.[3]

This was well understood until the twelfth century up to

which time Christ had been working intimately with the physical and etheric bodies of humanity. Because of this the deed of the Holy Communion was able to be fully comprehended.

> It was not widely discussed but was rather accepted in a manner that enabled one to feel that all was contained in the words, This is My body, and, This is My blood. Christ had indicated that he would be united with the earth, becoming its planetary Spirit. Because grain is the physical earth's most precious produce, bread became for man the body of Christ: the sap flowing through the plants became something from His blood.[4]

The perpetually moving blood, which is the expression of the human ego, is also the blood of sacrifice. But also blood is a substance which constantly wishes to become spiritual and pass beyond the confines of the material world. It must therefore be constantly destroyed and recreated so we can retain it within us. But after Christ's deed of sacrificing the blood it has a different quality, it has become the nourishment that the Grail knights found from the Holy Grail and becomes the blood of love.

If we consider Raphael's painting of the Madonna and Child *(Madonna del Prato)* in the Vienna Kunsthistorischemuseum, we can see this vividly depicted. The blood of the sacrifice is in the poppies behind the figures and the wild strawberries in the foreground. They are transient and frail, and therefore an ephemeral phenomenon as were the drops of physical blood that were shed. The red of Mary's gown has a much stronger hue and shines as if her feeling life is imbued with warmth and permanence. If one looks closely at the embroidery round the neck one can see a small golden inverted acanthus. This image was used in ancient Greek times to express their experience of the etheric world where it was usually presented reaching upward, showing the diffusion of the individual's etheric forces into the etheric world after death. Raphael has however inverted it to show the incarnation, the descent into the blood which can transform one's ego. This is the mission of blood that points to the future rather than the past:

> That which is to make all humanity one is no longer to depend upon the blood which pulsates in the "I." Therefore the superfluous "I"-blood flows through the wounds of Christ. All egoistic, self-seeking blood which unites a man with mother, father, brother, sister — all this has to flow! This is the real fact! With the amount of blood which flows there is lost the tendency to form limited communities, and there originates the tendency for the whole humanity to be united into one great community. When we learn to understand it in this way, we shall see the deepest purpose of Christianity is to unloose that which binds mankind within narrow limits. It will split up mankind into individuals who feel themselves to be separate, and who unite again in love of their own free will.[5]

In the plunging down gesture of Mithras, that sheds the fruitful blood, the incarnating ego can be seen with its attendant sacrifice and pain. In Raphael's Madonna, with her arms tenderly but emphatically lowered to her child in a gesture of support, the descending ego is again visible, but because of its blood-warm love it can accept the sacrifice as a path to something higher.

References

The following are quotations from Rudolf Steiner:
1. *Aspects of Ancient Wisdom in Early Christianity,* April 15, 1921.
2. *Building Stones for an Understanding of the Mystery of Golgotha,* April 10, 1917.
3. *Materialism and the Task of Anthroposophy,* June 3, 1921.
4. *Christianity in the Evolutionary Course of Mankind,* February 15, 1909.
5. *Festivals of the Seasons,* March 25, 1907.

Other sources:
Bahn and Verhut. *Images of the Ice Age.*
Cumont, F. *The Mysteries of Mithras.*
Godwin, Joscelyn. *Mystery Religion.*
Legge, F. *Forerunners and Rivals of Christianity.*
Schütze, Alfred. *Mithras.*
Steiner, R. *The Gospel of St John,* May 23, 1908.
—, *Study of Man,* August 23, 1919.

Of Blood and Money

Christopher Houghton Budd

Theoretical economics, shot through with mechanistic thinking, tends to be static in its methods and concepts: the price mechanism, money as a store of value. The language that has accompanied the actual use of money, however, is permeated by fluid analogies: currency, cash flow, liquidity, circulating capital — even sunk costs. It is, therefore, neither a new nor radical thought to consider money, as this article endeavours to do, in terms of circulation.

Likening money to blood, for example, clearly implies such a notion. And those conversant with Rudolf Steiner's lectures on economics will be familiar with his sketches of the economic process depicted in circular form.[1] But the analogy with blood is not as straightforward as it seems. The following remarks, though both tentative and primitive, are shared in order to highlight the problem of using such analogies in economics.

Where Rudolf Steiner has spoken of the heart — the organ people most readily associate with the blood — he has spoken of the need to see it not as a pump so much as an hydraulic ram.[2] The point being that the heart is activated by the flow of blood, the reverse of the usually held idea that the heart causes the blood to flow. Victor Bott and others have followed this idea up to demonstrate how the circulation, or rather the flow, of the blood precedes the beating of the heart. The heart's beat thus expresses the passage of blood into and out of it, not the other way round.

Herein, however, an important distinction needs to be noted between the idea of circulation, in the sense of going round, and that of the blood expanding away from and contracting back into the heart.

> The blood circulation does not really have the circuit-like arrangement often drawn in explanatory diagrams, although, functionally, blood follows the double, systemic/pulmonary circuits. ... The branches of the arterial and venous trees are actually, like trees, volume-filling.[3]

These trees are as if superimposed on one another, parallel; yet "delicate capillary networks [link their] peripheral branches ..."[4] Thus the blood passes from the heart out to the periphery via the arteries, then crosses over at the tips into the veins, whence it returns to the heart.

It also travels back and forth between the systemic and pulmonary aspects of the body, linking the metabolism and nerve-sense systems.

> The cycle of flowing movement in its completeness and rhythmically repeated continuity is almost beyond imagination; the heart itself a gath-

ering point for the blood. Each single ventricle-full of blood has returned from the microscopically fine, widely diffuse network of billions of capillaries: of the lungs, on the one hand, or of the entire body ... on the other. Each is passing on its way towards a state of microscopic dispersion in capillaries once more: this time through the entire body or through the entire lungs, respectively.[5]

In other words, the blood does not go round the body, but rays in and out within it. Though a useful brake on the unchecked progress of mechanistic thinking, therefore, the idea of circulation, when applied to money, in itself is only partially real. It is an attempt to go beyond materialistic thinking, but not proof of having done so. The analogy of money and blood circulation is one that should be used with care, therefore. The truer analogy is between money and the twin-directional flow of blood towards and away from the heart. It should be noted at this point that analogies do not proceed directly. Their important element is the imagery they suggest, pictures that bridge between similar phenomena in dissimilar realms — in this case, the circulation of the blood and money.

Within the processes of its ebb and flow, the blood also comes into being and goes out of being. Might it be in a similar sense that Rudolf Steiner spoke of the birth and death, youth and dying of money?[6] The idea of dying money has long exercised the minds of those seeking to understand Steiner's approach to economics, especially when trying to comprehend what such an idea means in practice. Could it be that this difficulty presents itself when one's image is of money going round the economy? On the other hand, as a thinkable thought the birth and death of money are far less problematical when one imagines money passing to and fro between the centre and the periphery of the economy.

Lineal thinking cannot understand such a notion, of course. In respect of living things, lineal thinking can at best attempt crude, and often erroneous, approximations. Circulation provides a case in point. Since the economy, and more especially the economic process, are living things — demanding living thinking — lineal thinking has to give way. One needs to realize that its approximations of living processes are really only useful as stepping stones, if such an image may be permitted, across the abyss that separates lineal and non-lineal thinking. They enable one to recognize the inadequacy of materialistic thinking in regard to money. As Kilner so aptly observes: "[The] aim is appreciation of the reality, which, if only it could be seen, would be absolutely breathtaking."[7]

To real economic thinking, in the sense that Rudolf Steiner used the term, the idea of money circulating round within a closed system is understandable but unsatisfactory. The same phenomenon — circulation — can also be understood, but better so, on the basis of money expanding and contracting from centre to periphery. But the ranging of money to and fro also suggests something of a higher order: the breathing of the economy. In the human organism the heart's beat is intimately connected to respiration, expressing the relationship between the blood and the lungs, representative respectively of the metabolism and the nervous system. The heart itself, linking blood and lungs, thus represents the rhythmic system, the harmonizer of the organism.

It is also on the passing back and forth of the blood that the human ego depends for its earthly existence, spanning thereby the poles of thinking and willing. The respiration of money between the centre and the periphery of the economy similarly provides a vehicle for human consciousness to enter into the economic process at every point and at every moment. "Without money it is absolutely impossible for human intelligence to enter in and play its part in the economic organism."[8] But where are the centre and the periphery of the economy? And what form do they take? Where is the "heart" and where the "skin" of the economic process, between which money passes to and fro?

Perhaps in Steiner's terms the heart of the economy is the point — never meant physically, of course — at which true price arises.

> A "true price" is forthcoming when a person receives, as counter-value for the product he has made, sufficient to enable him to satisfy the whole of his needs, including of course the needs of his dependants, until he will again have completed a like product.[9]

When a true price arises the disparities and discrepancies between values throughout the economy are resolved: reciprocation occurs and equilibrium is achieved — the goal of all economics. Here is not the place to go into how Rudolf Steiner envisaged true price being observed and given practical expression — that would entail a lengthy discussion of what he meant by associative economics. It is pertinent only to draw attention to the importance he attached to the idea of "true price."

The concept of true price also points to the skin of the economy. When Steiner speaks of true price in connection with needs and products, he is clearly pointing to the workings of economy — that is, to the production, distribution and consumption of values. This however is the domain of the economic process, the realm of commodification, about which Steiner says that three things are conventionally understood as commodities when in fact they are not: land, labour and capital. By arguing that land, labour and capital are not factors of production, as classical economics term them, but factors of price formation,[10] Steiner is making land, labour and capital the boundaries of the economy, its skin. Technically, the proper treatment (including their remuneration) of land, labour and capital proceeds when all three are understood as matters of right. The fact that they are rights and not commodities is simply masked by the practice of acquiring those rights by purchase and sale.

Economic life, though bounded by rights, is not determined by them; nor is it determined by the reciprocation of values. Both the creation of appropriate rights and reciprocal management of the economy are activities of the ego, of human consciousness. Working through the heart and skin of the economy in this way, human consciousness can be brought to bear upon the economic process. In so doing, it can provide that process with the boundaries, so necessary to economic and social health, that it is unable to provide itself. In this way, too, one can understand Steiner's remark that "with the economic process we always come to the human being. We can do no other than place him into the process [every time]."[11] (To such an approach, of course, the idea of market forces stands opposed.)

I am aware that Rudolf Steiner says more than once that economic relationships cannot be seen by the individual alone and that in practice this relies on associative working — combined consideration and assessment of economic life by the whole range of actors involved. Nevertheless Steiner's approach presupposes that people who thus work together are individually capable of economic thinking; able, that is, to speak the language of economics. It is to this greatly underestimated task that these remarks are addressed. Deliberately so, they imply a field of research considerably beyond the scope of this article and thus risk giving the impression of being ungrounded. This is not to say that they cannot be grounded, however. Seminal thoughts normally precede their verification, and I have expressed my contribution in this way in part to invite criticism and elaboration of it.

I have another reason: the demands of economic thinking are easily underestimated, and what spiritual science reveals is all too readily confused with materialist ideas which, while apparently similar, are in fact in contest. Epistemologically speaking, today's challenge is not to extend materialism so that it explains the non-material world, but to understand unseen realities sufficiently concretely that they also explain the realm of matter. Economics, which is wholly concerned with invisible realities, is peculiarly affected by this fact. As great a test as any of spiritual science's efficacy in this respect concerns the light it can shed on the nature of money. The distinction between money going round and its being an expression of the economy's respiration provides, if not a measure, at least an illustration of the potency of spiritual scientific economics, as well as the distance we have yet to travel in bringing it about.

References
1. Steiner, R. *Economics,* New Economy Publications, 1993. *See pull-out flap.*
2. Steiner, R. *Spiritual Science and Medicine,* Rudolf Steiner Press, London 1975, quoted in Bott, V. *Anthroposophical Medicine,* Rudolf Steiner Press, 1978.
3. Kilner, P. "Our Heart," in *Chaos, Rhythm and Flow: The Golden Blade No.46,* Floris Books, 1993, p.51.
4. *Ibid.* p.33.
5. Kilner, P. *The Developing Heart,* Flow Design Research Group, Emerson College, 1983, p.14.
6. See Steiner, R. *Economics,* Lecture 12.
7. Kilner, P. "Our Heart," *(op.cit.)* p.53.
8. Steiner, R. *Economics, (op.cit.)* p.66.
9. *Ibid.* p.83.
10. *Ibid.* Lecture 7.
11. *Ibid.* pp.126, 128.

Money — the Christ-Blood of the Threefold Social Order

Jack Foster

From Archetypal to Fundamental Social Law

In the statement at the front of this journal — *The Golden Blade* — we find the oft-quoted words describing anthroposophy: "A path of knowledge, to guide the spiritual in the human being to the spiritual in the universe."[1]

This path of knowledge, a path to freedom, carries with it the danger of alienation and isolation.

> If human fellowship is not achieved, all talk of occult development is empty.[2]

> Christianity must be inwardly experienced, for it is the opposite pole to the experience of freedom, which must emerge. Freedom must be experienced, but the experience of freedom along would lead human beings into the abyss. Only the Mystery of Golgotha can lead man across this abyss.[3]

The path to freedom was initiated by the gods; the path to brotherhood, the bridge from human to human, is in the hands of Man himself, as a fruit of his freedom.

One of the major contributions of Rudolf Steiner was the Threefold Commonwealth:

> The proposals for the Threefold Social Order are the Christianity of today; they are spiritual revelations clothed in external forms.[4]

> Bourgeois culture is on the decline ... whereas we are witnessing the dawn of another culture which is largely not understood and is represented by the proletariat. ... What we call Spiritual Science, or Anthroposophy, we have for some time considered to be the true spiritual foundation of what today is on the ascent.[5]

This practical external aspect of anthroposophy was first given form by Rudolf Steiner in the Fundamental Social Law:

> In a community of human beings working together, the less the individual claims for himself the fruits of his own work, and the more of these fruits he makes over to his fellow-workers, satisfying his own requirements from the work which they have done, the greater will be the well-being of the community.[6]

The Fundamental Social Law was given as the Foundation Stone of external anthroposophy, that is, of the Threefold Social Order, even before the Christmas

Meeting of 1923 planted the Foundation Stone of the General Anthroposophical Society into the hearts of its members.

Nearly two thousand years earlier, marking the transition from "divine commandment" to "human law," the Christ had given the archetypal Social Law: *Thou shalt love thy neighbour as thyself.*

In confirmation of this new consciousness, Christ told the parable of the labourers in the vineyard, giving expression to the universal human, to human worth and to the essential equality of human beings: "I will give unto this last, even as unto thee."

In 1905, Rudolf Steiner gave voice to the evolution of the consciousness soul (which has given us natural science, the industrial revolution, the division of labour, and the economic sphere of the social order) by establishing, in the Fundamental Social Law, the principle of economic life today — that of altruism, compassion and love.

Associative consciousness for a new social order

How is this new social consciousness to take effect? Rudolf Steiner gave indications for the formation of new social organs of consciousness — "associations" — through which the Fundamental Social Law can become effective. Why associations? Because as far as the economic life is concerned, the individual human being lacks the capacity to make sound judgements — "any individual judgement is a false one" — for the simple reason that the human being exists within the economic organism, and the objective onlooker consciousness which is the hallmark of the consciousness soul age is ineffectual.

> In the economic life man must associate with others; for what one man does not know, another may know. The individual consciousness of one man vanishes in association with others. ... Where human soul-life disappears in an unconscious sphere, love must spread over the associative life, and love is an element of the will. Love, an element of the will, must permeate economic life; brotherliness must permeate economic life.[7]

An element of sacrifice must enter in. In the democratic life of feeling, individual consciousness is submerged in the folk consciousness, while in the economic field of the will, it submerges into the whole world economy.

Formed out of the threefold nature of the human being as manifest in the economic processes of production, marketing and consumption, associations become vehicles of corporate imaginations; ordering the economic transubstantiation of the earth, striving to create a temple for the human universal, and establishing a springboard for the individual's reconnection with the spiritual in the universe. The associative impulse, the fruit of consciousness soul development, is summed up by Rudolf Steiner as follows:

> What matters is this vital dealing with men and women, this allowing the whole social order to originate from the insight of Associations.[8]

> It is a mistake that makes people say constantly:

"to realize the threefold order, human beings must be different than they are now." No! Through the threefold order, people will be educated in such a way that they will grow up to be different than they were previously under the economic state.[9]

As a result of the associations created simply out of the economic life the initiative of the individual will be maintained.[10]

And the motto of the social ethic:

The healthy social life is found when in the mirror of each human soul the whole community finds its reflection, and when in the community the virtue or uniqueness of each one is living.[11]

The etherization/redemption of money

In associations, the new social consciousness is promoted, while the integrity of the individuality is safeguarded and fostered. And so to the vital question: What instruments are at hand with which the associations can effectively balance and regulate the three spheres of the social order?

For the answer to this question we must return once more to the life of Christ. *The Fifth Gospel* relates how Ahriman tried to entrap the Christ with the temptation to turn stones into bread; how Christ's response was circumscribed by His lack of knowledge of the future earthly conditions in which money (stones) would indeed by exchanged for bread; how because this temptation could not be fully overcome at the time, Judas became the vessel through which Ahriman could betray the Christ for thirty pieces of silver.

The betrayal of Christ for thirty pieces of silver has been redeemed and metamorphosed. The coming of the etheric Christ in this century has enabled the Ahrimanic temptation to be vanquished — with miraculous results. We see the forces of the etheric Christ penetrating into and working within the life-blood of the social order — that most esoteric substance of money.

Rudolf Steiner describes how in the contemporary economic process of buying and selling — which, of necessity, is based on a "natural egotism," since one's own survival is at stake — every participant makes a gain, or profit. For the transaction would not take place at all if this impulse for self-satisfaction was lacking. In this process of exchange, necessitated by the extreme specialization of the division of labour, profit or surplus value is created. This surplus value, accumulated as capital, is the basis upon which all spiritual/cultural activity is made possible. In a community economy every individual is instrumental in this process of the creation of capital, which in turn serves the fulfilment of each individual destiny.

What is it that has happened here? Christ, in taking upon himself the sins or karma of humankind in so far as it affects the world in which we live, has transformed the essential individual egotism of Man's natural existence into the creative altruistic community substance of capital.

We read, in "The Etherization of the Blood," how:

> human blood, which is a physical substance, perpetually resolves itself into etheric substance, so that in the region of heart a continual transformation of the blood into fine etheric substances takes place ...
>
> ... Something similar to that which has been described for the microcosm takes place also in the macrocosm. ... Just as our blood streams upwards as ether from the heart, so since the Mystery of Golgotha the etherized blood of Christ Jesus has lived in the ether of the earth. ... Since the Mystery of Golgotha a possibility has continually existed, that the action of the etheric blood of Christ might take part in these currents from below upwards.
>
> ... A union of the human bloodstream with the bloodstream of Christ Jesus can, however, only come to pass when people bring a right understanding towards what is contained in the Christ Impulse.

And then we read:

> All that can be gained in the way of external progress, or in the mastery of the forces of nature, is but small and insignificant compared with what will be given to the man who has experienced in his soul an awakening through the Christ Who is now entering into human civilization and into all its concerns. What men will attain through this are positive co-ordinating forces. Christ brings constructive forces into human civilization.[12]

It is with this background that we can experience the redemption and resurrection of money. The values which are created in the economic sphere enter into the life cycle of money, circulating through the political sphere of rights relationships, into the spiritual/cultural sphere. So we see this etheric movement — this life cycle — as the product of the economic processes involved in the transubstantiation of the earth; as the external image of a new linking ladder between heaven and earth; and as the creator of a "new unity, a higher community."

The Christ-blood of the social organism

As the earth has become the body of Christ, so have human relationships been imbued with the blood of Christ, active in that magical substance of money which Rudolf Steiner characterizes as the "spirit realized." But how are we to relate to this life-blood of the social order? What thoughts and images are required to enable us to use wisely this gift of the etheric Christ?

When we use it, either as individuals or in our institutions, do we stop to think whether our inspiration comes from Lucifer, Ahriman, or the Christ?

When we use it, are we aware of the qualitative differences of money, according to each stage of its life cycle? Do we distinguish between purchase, loan and gift, in the service of the physical, legal or cultural spheres?

Do we appreciate its "potential" character, recognizing that when freed from all encumbrances — in similar fashion to abstract thinking — it can serve the multifarious creativity of individual human beings?

Are we aware, as is the case with the blood in the human organism, of its sacrificial nature, able to forgo its own intrinsic value in order to serve any and each of the diverse destinies of human individualities?

Do we rejoice in the healing power of money, and of capital as the arbiter of "a higher unity, a new community"?

We may set up our own communities around school, farm or church. We may, in the process, eschew egotism and exercise self-sacrifice (and surely such communities of shared interests and common concerns are highly desirable), but we should forever bear in mind their links with, firstly, the supreme sacrifice of the Christ Being and, secondly, the working together of the whole human community. In taking on the karma of "natural egotism," the Christ redeemed money from its purely material aspect, enabling it to become the instrument of altruism, and to be freely given in the service of the spirit. In working with the division of labour — one of the fruits of the consciousness soul — the whole community participates in the creation of capital, while at the same time being already unconsciously working in the sense of the Fundamental Social Law. Do we appreciate — with this knowledge and understanding and with these thoughts continuously in mind (however circumscribed our action) — how different our own financial deliberations might be, and how much more fruitful may be the effects on our own institutions?

Finally, do we realize the cumulative effect that such creative thoughts might have in the ailing economy of the world at large?

Christ — the Ego of the associative organism

In addition to the regulation of the life cycle of money with all its ancillary aspects, such as we have just been discussing, a major function of associative consciousness is the formation of price:

> A "true price" is forthcoming when a person receives, as counter-value for the product he has made, sufficient to enable him to satisfy the whole of his needs, including of course the needs of his dependants, until he will again have completed a like product.
> ... Economic Science is precisely an understanding of how the whole economic process can be included in this formula.[13]

When we take the bare bones of this process of price formation, which reflects not only the altruistic nature of contemporary economy but also the essence of a Christ-community "where two or three, or many, are gathered together in my Name," we can see the following. Economic values arise out of the interaction of the three factors of production: land, labour and capital. Labour combined with nature/land creates a positive value V1, whereas labour organized and saved by spiritual activity capital (that is, by machinery, division of labour, and so on) lessens the value V2. From the interplay of these two values, price arises. It is through the regulation of these life-processes lying behind the outer factors of production; it is through the attention to human needs in price regulation; that associations fulfil

MONEY — THE CHRIST-BLOOD

their task. If we embrace this price-forming activity in a diagram we shall then see the crowning glory:

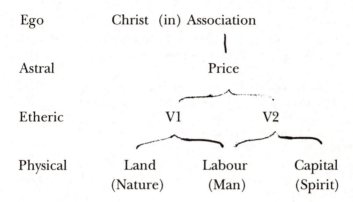

It was perhaps in this sense that Steiner spoke in a lecture on "The New Isis": "Those who work in economic associations will bring about a Christ-filled social order."[14]

These associative organs of a corporate consciousness — vehicles for the cosmic ego — must now be woven into the very fabric of society if the social impulses, which manifest in infinite variety today, are to be harnessed in a new Christ-centred social order; and if the travesty of market forces and other ego-inspired activities (for instance, the Stock Exchange and National Lottery) are to be superseded by the Christ-redeemed power of money — the Christ-blood of the social order. Only so can community-generated capital fulfil its task of serving the spiritual destiny of every individual as well as the mission of humankind.

References

The following are all quotations from Rudolf Steiner:
1. *Anthroposophical Leading Thoughts,* I, February 17, 1924.
2. "At the Gates of Spiritual Science," Lecture II, Stuttgart, September 1, 1906.
3. *Cosmosophy,* Vol.I, Dornach, October 16, 1921.
4. "Some Characteristics of Today," Heidenheim, June 12, 1919.
5. "A Social Basis for Primary and Secondary Education," Stuttgart 1919.
6. "Anthroposophy and the Social Question," Lucifer-Gnosis, 1905/6.
7. "The Threefold Nature of the Human Organism," Dornach, November 27, 1920.
8. "World Economy," Lecture 6, Dornach, July 29, 1922.
9. *Renewal of the Social Organism,* Rudolf Steiner Press 1985.
10. Three Lectures on the Social Question, Oxford 1922.
11. Inscribed in Edith Maryon's copy of *The Threefold Social Order,* November 1920.
12. October 1, 1911, Basel.
13. "World Economy," Lecture 6, Dornach, July 29, 1922.
14. "The Search for the New Isis," Dornach, December 25, 1920.

Chosen Destiny

Rudi Lissau

The provocative situation in which I was once asked how an anthroposophist could incarnate as a Jew prompted me to answer: "One of the advantages might be to have been spared the ministrations of the traditional churches."

I am intensely aware of the fact that I, born in 1911, was able to incarnate in a family deeply devoted to Rudolf Steiner. Never was there a time in my life in which I was not conscious of the existence of this unique man. My father and his brother — the latter to become the first secretary of the Goetheanum in the first years of the creation of this building — were among the eight people who early in the century founded the Theosophical Society in Vienna in order to provide a platform for Rudolf Steiner's activity in Austria.

Both my father and my mother were Jews, but father had already moved away from Judaism, while mother when she married was a liberal agnostic. It was a time when the problem of race had acquired a real fascination for "modern" people — today we might rather argue in terms of differing cultures or of sociological groups — and father had come under the influence of Otto Weininger, a brilliant young Jew who was filled by a hatred of women and a hatred of Jews. Father was also misled by Steiner's great respect for German culture, not seeing that this respect applied to the age of Goethe, Novalis and the German idealistic philosophers, and unaware that Steiner had no truck with the nationalism and imperialism of Wilhelminian Germany.

But, typically for a Jew, however great his distance from Jewish life and Jewish religion became, he took no outward step towards separation from his ancestral religion in order not to hurt his parents. Only after their deaths could we openly and joyously celebrate Christmas. Until then we were simply spectators at the celebration of the Christian members of our household.

So my experience of Jewish religion was fairly remote. Once or twice a year I was sent to the synagogue, a rather embarrassing experience, while the religion lessons in school were simply a bore. But I enjoyed the occasional invitations to the Passover meal in the house of a rabbi, a personal friend of my father's. Such a meal is a family affair to which a few guests are invited and as the youngest member at the table I enjoyed a particular position. The meal is permeated by a truly human mood. Its ambience is not easy to describe for me as it is composed of different, indeed almost contradictory elements. A ritual, centuries old, and spontaneous light conversation and gentle humour and laughter, reminiscences and introspection, human warmth and devotion to God, the memory of past sufferings, the gratitude for having been spared during the last year. Paramount the undying hope: "This year here, next year in Jerusalem."

As an adolescent I had taken a position not much

different from that of many liberal Austrian Jews. I was not interested in Jewish religion and Jewish life. I was an Austrian, though occasionally handicapped by my Jewish ancestry. I shared the general dislike of Eastern European Jews in their distinct and alien attire who, unsettled by the First World War and its aftermath, came to Austria in large numbers. These were the people, I believed, who caused anti-semitism. In other words, I had adopted a typically xenophobic attitude. We, of course, are alright, but these people — whoever they might be — are inferior to us. Their habits, their morals, their outward behaviour make them deeply suspect. I did not want to have anything to do with them. Life was to teach me different.

In my early twenties I became a teacher of blind children and for five years worked and lived among blind people. The institute which became my home was a relic of the Austro-Hungarian Empire. Our pupils came from thirteen different countries, particularly from Eastern Europe, many from Jewish homes. They showed me how distorted my preconceptions of Eastern European Jews were. Instead of a type, I came in touch with individuals who showed as much variety of behaviour and appearance as "we Austrians."

My blind pupils, many of them to become victims of the Holocaust, gave me an invaluable present: they freed me from my feeling of inferiority as a Jew. From now on my Jewish heredity was as much a karmic fact as my sanguine temperament, it had advantages and disadvantages, and was nothing to be embarrassed about. More important, they conveyed to me that the mood I had encountered at the Passover meals was not a once-in-a-blue-moon phenomenon, but the climax of a basic attitude which permeated every aspect of life throughout the cycle of the year.

Throughout the Fifties I was friends with a charming man, a Catholic Rhinelander by birth, but an anthroposophist and music teacher at the Basel Steiner school. A truly religious man he had left the Roman Church. Neither The Christian Community met his needs nor the esoteric School. But he felt a close kinship to the religious meditations of Eastern European Jews. His library contained many books of stories of Chassidic rabbis, their deliberations and meditations. They opened a new world to me: traditional Jewish piety nurtured a contemporary German in a way which neither traditional Christianity nor Rudolf Steiner whom he deeply appreciated could give him. The intense Love of God of these rabbis and their disciplined endeavour to fathom His mind in their meditations opened up to me a new dimension of Jewish life. Where else in Europe were there lay people — a rabbi is not a priest — with such a concern with questions of justice, of piety, of morality, of the good life? Where were other large groups of people for whom God mattered to this extent?

A third experience came in the seventies and eighties. In my work at the Wynstones Kindergarten Training Course I encountered a number of most interesting students from Israel. In their intellectual and religious dilemma concerning the central position of the New Christianity in Steiner's work they naturally turned to me hoping I could empathize with their predicament.

Through them I realized that their existential position was utterly different from that of former generations of Central and Eastern European Jews. They had a state, they were a nation, they had to come to terms with the reality of power. The inner glory and the outer tragedy of European Jewry had been — and possibly still is — their utter insecurity. They exemplified two general human truths: I live by the ministrations of those around me; and: the human Ego grows out of our own inner resources and out of our inner relation to God in His world of the Spirit.

One of our difficulties when looking at a religion other than our own is that we presume they all hold practically the same beliefs, share a common form of life, and are utterly different from other confessional communities. So we fasten a particular label on a group of people, a dangerous attitude as I had found out in my prejudice concerning Eastern European Jews. What have "born-again Christians" of the southern States in common with Irish Catholics? What unites Zen Buddhists and Burmese generals, Tibetan lamas and followers of the "Living Buddha" in Japan? After the death of the founder, religious movements tend to split and splinter. Buddha gave us the Eightfold Path. Steiner recreated it in a modern, western way. Compare his version in *Knowledge of Higher Worlds* with the formulation of modern Zen. The result may be utter bewilderment.

On the other hand many religions arrive at an orthodoxy with clearly formulated tenets, and contain at the same time forms of mysticism, ecstatic movements and other forms of religious life not too dissimilar from those of other religions. One of my former pupils married a Bengali Hindu. The first-born was a son. Granny in Calcutta felt she had to fly to England to make sure that an equivalent to our baptism was celebrated, and celebrated in the most appropriate manner.

The English grandfather, a religious man and an anthroposophist, asked to be present at the ceremony. He was anxious to experience the full depth of a religious act that arose in pre-Christian times, the living manifestation of an utterly different, more spiritual consciousness. He was bitterly disappointed. No religious experience, no emotional depth, simply a traditional ritual carried out to the letter. But this is exactly the attitude for which the orthodox Jew is blamed. As long as everything is properly carried out the success of a religious rite is assured. The participants need not experience great emotional depths, the celebrant need not be a person of outstanding morality. The Roman as well as the Orthodox churches look at the Eucharist as an *opus operatum,* a deed completed long ago, and independent of the morality of the celebrant.

Each religion is lived in a wide variety of life styles and — as my own experience as an adolescent taught me — it is only too easy to typecast one particular form of behaviour as characteristic for the whole group. How often have I heard in Austria "if only all Jews were like you" or "like your family," particularly from people who had hardly ever met another Jew. One learned to accept such a statement and hoped that life would teach the person concerned to rise above his or her preconceptions. As long as we do not wean ourselves from typecasting the alien, as Shylocks or Fagins, how can we be numbered among the followers of Christ as Steiner presented him: He came to all mankind, but to each one individually. To speak of Christian nations is a misunderstanding.

This situation is complicated by the belief that the Jews are the Chosen People whom God bound to Himself in a sacred covenant. Through the way they lead their lives, through their suffering they testify to the relevance of this Covenant. This gives the religious Jew a feeling of superiority, sometimes even of arrogance. Like the Cathars of the Languedoc they are not surprised that the "world" is evil. Their conviction makes them look at the "world" as something rather inferior, and the Covenant depends on maintaining a purity of blood.

This special and unique relationship to God results in a religious intensity unknown to most modern Christians. Every act of daily life is a sacred act. The householder wakes up and immediately walks to the window. He looks outside. Does nature look the same or has overnight the Messiah come? No food is taken without a grace being said, and there is a vast number of graces. There is one, say, for eating oranges, and a special grace for eating the first orange of the season.

The occult day, as Steiner confirms, begins at nightfall on the previous evening. For the Jew, then, the climax of the week is Friday evening, the eve of the Sabbath. I have not forgotten what Hannah told me. Among my blind pupils she was the gentlest as well as the most gifted, almost certainly a victim of the Holocaust. Her family was pitifully poor and hunger was not uncommon. But every Friday night there was the Meal, celebrated in peace and joy, and amidst thanks to God for the food the family were able to eat in this, the first hour of the Sabbath. The small girl realized that the week's diet had to be kept to a minimum so that Friday could be celebrated in a dignified way.

When I see the Oberufer Three Kings Play I am very sensitive to the way in which the Jewish priests have been told to handle the Bible scrolls. Like the breviary of the priest in The Christian Community these scrolls are handwritten. In the synagogue three passages are read from the Bible and it is deemed a great honour if a person is chosen to read one of today's passages to the congregation. Whoever handles the scroll will do so with greatest care and his first act will be to kiss it. When the scroll becomes fragile with age it is not assigned to the waste paper basket, it is not even burned. God's word is given a proper funeral and is ritually buried. In present-day Israel, orthodox Jews speak Yiddish. How could you demean Hebrew, the language which God spoke, by using it when buying a bus ticket?

But it would be entirely erroneous to assume the Jewish piety and devotion exhausts itself in ritual practices, however appropriate and dignified. Although the intensity of the religious and spiritual life of the individual is not unique to Jewish life, the circumstances are unusual. For the spiritual activity takes place not in an *ashram* in a lonely Himalayan valley, but in a normal household which forms a protective mantle around the seeker for God, and its aim is only incidentally a mystic union. It has practical aims: how to solve a moral dilemma, how to advise a person in need, how to become a better person, how to increase God's kingdom on earth. In this specific sense Jewish life is unique. God's "command" to Abraham that his descendants should be a folk of priests finds its fulfilment in two ways: first, that the Jew is encouraged not to follow the commands of a priestly hierarchy, but to learn to act individually. Secondly, the realization that we are endowed for this work in different degrees and so we respect and support those who are best able to carry out this "command." So we see as one of the central realizations of Jewish culture the intense seeker of enlightenment who attempts to fathom some fragment of the mind of God and to appreciate its consequences for our moral and social life. Such a man is accompanied by a band of disciples, supported by a group of helpers, and respected by a much wider community. Jewish lore treasures the achievements of such individuals over long stretches of time. It is aware of knowledge that arose out of the total commitment of individuals, and understands that spiritual knowledge is personal and therefore multi-faceted.

Mention should be made here of two particular forms of Jewish religious life. First, the Chassidim, a movement (if I am not mistaken) only a couple of centuries old, the roots of which may well be buried in much older layers of Jewish culture. Chassidic Jews stress our emotional commitment to God which has priority over the strict ritual insisted on by the orthodox Jew. The man filled with the love of God is so full of joy that he will sing and dance. Much of Chassidic religious insight and experience speaks to us in the works of Martin Buber. People acquainted with Steiner are often strongly attracted by Buber's stories and absolutely amazed that "this man is not even a Christian, leave alone an anthroposophist."

The occult treasures of the Cabbala are widely recognized. According to Professor Maurin it antedates the book of Genesis and is the precious relic of the insights of people who still lived very close to the Divine World and its beings. Steiner knew that Cabbala and in a number of places used images and concepts of this primeval lore. Today the teachings of the Cabbala have fertilized much occult thinking, but in the first half of our century when Cabbalistic knowledge was still confined to a small circle, the greatest living scholar of the Cabbala was Ernst Müller, one of the founders of the Vienna Theosophical Society. He emigrated to England where he was held in greatest esteem by George Adams who discussed occult as well as mathematical problems with him.

We shall now turn to Steiner. The picture of Jahve which Blavatsky had given to theosophists was definitely negative: a harsh, judgmental, stern deity. But by 1911 Steiner had so far moved away from theosophical ideas that he was able, in Berlin on 13 March, to make the bold statement that Jahve is *wesensgleich* with Christ. "*Wesensgleich*" is not a word generally used, but its most basic translation would be "identical." But it would seem best not to go for a hard-and-fast word at all. Just as the Divine Father and the Divine Son are aspects of the same Divinity so Jahve and Christ are manifestations of the same Being at different stages of His approach to human perception.

What Jahve revealed to Abraham and, at a later stage, to Moses forged together an often recalcitrant people who were to provide the body of the incarnate God, as well as, particularly in the work of the Prophets, the concepts and images through which He could reveal Himself to earthly human beings.

Steiner is not so much interested in what Christ said, but in what He did. As I understand it, each statement of the Sermon on the Mount had already been said by one or the other Jewish prophet who preceded Christ by two or three centuries. Readers of Steiner's lecture on the Lord's Prayer may have felt disappointed that he did not dwell on the moral implications of these verses. But Steiner looks at the actual situation: Christ addresses a group of Jews. They know already in advance each statement in proportion to the degree in which they had opened themselves to the riches of their prophetic tradition. Steiner shows in this lecture how Christ selected those statements of this tradition which He could weave into a verbal texture revealing the fullness of the human being as a spiritual-physical totality.

   Jahve and Christ: the "One" chose Abraham and bade him assemble around him people, each one of them able to become a priest, to learn to take on individual responsibility and not to live the life of tribal masses subject to the will and whim of a superhuman king, the Son of Heaven. Jewish myth puts the position of Abraham, newly endowed with individual responsibility, into an impressive picture: he was the first man whose hair turned white. But the "Other" widened this challenge to embrace every human being, and died for all, that is for each human individuality. At first there was a relation from God to one chosen man who then conveyed this experience to the rest of the people chosen. But Christ works without a mediator. He approaches each one of us individually when He recognizes our potential to receive Him. Between these two distinct relationships stand historically the Jewish prophets. The last of them was John who witnessed the union of Christ and Jesus of Nazareth.

   We can contemplate the close relationship of Jahve and Christ also by pondering the importance of the Meal. I mentioned the unique position, dignity and joy of the meal on Friday night. I recounted the impression which the Passover meal made on the little boy who had hardly any idea of what happened around him, but still was able to deeply appreciate the mood of this very special meal. And this was the meal which Christ hallowed and lifted up to establish the Eucharist and to lay the foundation, in word and deed, for the second half of the history of this planet, a process described by the orthodox churches as the Deification of Man.

Steiner welcomed the presence of Jews in Europe and hoped that the host nations would be liberal enough to open their societies to their Jewish fellow citizens so that the latter would gradually completely merge with their hosts. Conversely, he was perturbed by the beginning of Zionism. It reduced the importance of the Jews for the development of mankind. They had become a people spread over the whole globe and were in a position to accelerate the growing awareness of the spiritual unity of mankind, an essentially Christian impulse. Zionism however pointed them in the opposite direction, into nationhood and nationalism. The future was to show how justified his apprehension had been.

I now turn to specific remarks which Steiner made in Vienna. It was probably in the early Twenties that he said there he was unable to discuss two subjects because he was painfully aware of the consequences of his words on the emotions of his audience: human sexuality and anti-semitism.

When an anthroposophist of long standing and a man with a Jewish background asked: "What is the task of the modern Jew?" Steiner answered thereby the question which this article posed at the beginning, and the answer is momentous: "His task is to spiritualize Christianity which the Catholic Church has Ahrimanized and the Protestants intellectualized."

If we look at the quest of the modern Israeli we see that the majority of Israelis are Sephardim, Jews who had lived in Muslim empires. So they are ignorant of traditional Christianity, but also mainly untouched by antisemitism because the Prophet had imbued his followers with respect for the "people of the Book." The emergence of the state of Israel — to a certain extent also the Balfour declaration — created terrible tension between Muslims and Jews, mainly in the political and not the religious field.

The European Jews who were the founding fathers of the state of Israel had been always in close proximity to Christianity. For them it had been impossible to remain indifferent. Some were filled with a secret longing for Christ, while others felt real hatred for Him. An outstanding example of the former group is Shalom Asch. This great writer in Yiddish wrote a most interesting trilogy. *The Nazarene* describes the life of Christ according to the gospel of Judas which two men find early in the twentieth century. Judas had recognized the Christ, but realizing his divine power betrayed him in the expectation that He would now be forced to use his power and liberate the Jews from the Roman yoke. The second part of the trilogy is called *The Apostle*, that is, Paul, and the third part *The Mother*, the Virgin Mary.

But as far as I can probe little is left in contemporary Israel either of the secret longing for Christ or of hatred. So it might seem that there is little left in contemporary Jewish awareness of a connection to Christ. This is particularly important as today definite efforts are under way at the Goetheanum to move the Anthroposophical Society from a Central European society into a multicultural one of global dimension.

This will be a formidable task and one for which we have little experience. But my work with young Israelis at the Wynstones Kindergarten Training Course makes me think that among them will be a sizeable number who will find Christ in a modern way, free from conventional shackles. Some will be stirred by contact with anthroposophical life. But the grace of Christ can awaken any human being, and in such a case it is only a question of finding the conceptual framework to explain the moment of recognition. There is only one other culture which before the Incarnation prepared the ground for an understanding of the Mystery of Golgotha in any way that approximates to the contribution of the Hebrew people. The ancient Greeks had given to the world the profound and intimate teaching of the Logos, the Divine Word which became the central conviction of the Gospel of St John.

The Jewish tradition offers us the story of the Fall, the selection of Abraham, the mission of Moses, Solomon's temple, the prophetic tradition, John the Baptist and many of the statements which Christ made to His Jewish followers. They form a sound enough basis for any modern Jew who has been touched by the Christ impulse to recognize in his experience most of the features which were dear to him in his own culture. Such a person need only make the step from the blood-bound tribal religion of the "chosen people" to the world-wide humanitarian impulse which imbued many European Jews from the Age of Enlightenment right into our own time. Such a person will be helped by one of Steiner's central insights, the changing human consciousness, the process at the heart of history.

As I survey the destinies of people whom I have met personally I conclude that a good part of anthroposophists who chose for their incarnation a Jewish background were filled with a deep longing for Christ, a longing which coloured their whole stance within anthroposophy. An outstanding figure in this context is Karl König. At the age of sixteen, years before he ever heard of Steiner he went to his father, a deeply religious Jew, and said: "Father, I am a Christian." He knew that this confession was bound to hurt deeply the father whom he respected. During his whole life König referred to his Jewish descent.

The respectful silence in Camphill House while König was meditating evoked the ethos of the Viennese tradition of muted voices and eager anticipation among the Rabbinical pupils while their teacher was intent on prayer and clarification. *"Der Rebbe klärt,"* is a phrase from stories and anecdotes understood by non-Jews and Jews alike. The characteristic centre of Camphill life, the Bible evening, no doubt is largely based on Tilla König's experience in Herrenhut. But it has equally strong connections to the Meal of Jewish tradition. König's biographer, Hans Müller-Wiedermann told me that for him writing this book arose out of his own deep striving for a new harmonization of German-Jewish relationships.

So I venture now to answer the question: Why should participants in the pre-natal school of Michael choose an incarnation in a Jewish surrounding? I admonish myself not to generalize for the ways of karma are most diverse and subtle. But it is my conviction that pupils of Michael in whose School, as Steiner tells us, the New Christianity formed the core of the "teaching" received could hardly have chosen a more direct way to the New Mysteries, the mysteries of Christ, than by spending their childhood and youth in a Jewish surrounding. Not only were they spared the ministrations of the traditional churches which caused in so many of our contemporaries indifference towards, and even contempt for Christianity, but in the Jews' concern for God and in their religious practice in daily life they acquired a basis for direct access to the Mystery of Golgotha and for a strong and individual religious life with or without a renewed Christian ritual. The Jew's endeavour to live his daily life as an act of devotion can lead directly to accept Steiner's challenge in the central meditation of the anthroposophist: "Practice, practice, practice."

Book reviews

Jenny Josephson

The Harmony of the Human Body. Musical Principles in Human Physiology, Armin J. Husemann. Floris Books. £19.99.

Why Me? Interviews with seven people with AIDS, Margje Koster. Floris Books. £6.99.

In recent thinking, art and science have become separate disciplines with little or no overlap or understanding of each other. Science has also long distanced itself from religion, from the divine, from the spirit. In this century, many of the arts have followed this path of separation as well; very little can truly be called sacred art. Thus the three great disciplines of art, science and religion which were once united in the ancient Mystery centres have become emancipated from each other, just as the human being in this century, having crossed the threshold to the spiritual world unconsciously in the will, has three areas of soul-life — thinking, feeling and willing — that are increasingly disunited. The tragedies and barrenness of these separated disciplines also reflect in human lives, leading to dissatisfaction and a need to break down barriers, even if not always the most appropriate ones. We cannot return to the old forms but we can move forward.

One of the greatest barriers to moving forward is the present day materialistic, scientific view of the human being. By the time young people start to face exam work (and even much before this), this way of thinking creeps in and clouds perception. The wonder of the human body in both structure and function — anatomy and physiology — is lost. Instead of being revered as a temple of the cosmos, the body is reduced to mechanistic principles: not so much the vehicle of the individual human soul and spirit, as on a level with the modern car.

These two books open doors for us to move forward. In *The Harmony of the Human Body,* Armin Husemann takes scientific and statistical data of the human being both in its development and in its organic parts, and transforms these data into artistic expression. The music of the spheres becomes visible, incarnated into the human body. The forming might of the Word is tentatively, carefully, shown in sculpture and movement.

The chapters are broken up into not too lengthy sections which makes it possible to dip in and taste the author's insights. As I read through, I found so many thoughts and pictures arising that the experience was almost like reading Grimm. Mechanistic thinking has a hard time here; an open thinking for the arts and spiritual science is needed. An excellent Christmas present for all artists, therapists and teachers who need to unify the art, science and religion of the human being in daily work and life — indeed for all interested in the "generally human," the Adam Kadman in each of us.

Why Me? is quite a different book, a rough diamond beside a polished one, dealing with the rawness of human lives. Whereas Armin Husemann discusses the arts in measured tones, this book is made up of human tapestries often roughly woven with knots and tangles but shot through with luminous threads and glints of gold. No measured tones or harmonies here, but rather the discord and the resolution of human lives and emotions. A book that brought tears to my eyes at the suffering and pain but also at the nobility that comes through. As they tell their own stories, the courage and insight of these individuals is humbling. There is also wonder for the phoenix-like quality of the human spirit as it rises from the ashes of a biography — indomitable and still striving on.

Many of these seven biographies answer their own question — Why me? — showing that even in our darkest moments, facing pain and death, we can find meaning, purpose and usefulness. Not only the conscious soul is at work here but seeds of the spirit self shine out, too, showing that AIDS is an illness of the future in all senses. This is a book for all who doubt the meaning of illness or consider it negative. Here illness is shown to be a healing force in itself.

Notes on the contributors

James Dyson practises medicine and is a director of the Park Attwood Clinic, Stourbridge.

Karal Jan Tusenius is a medical practitioner in Holland.

Andrew Welburn is a fellow of New College, Oxford, and author of several books on literature and the Mystery tradition.

Christopher Clouder is a Waldorf school teacher and teacher/trainer, and present chairman of the Steiner Schools Fellowship board.

Christopher Houghton Budd is a freelance economist, author and editor of *New Economy*.

Jack Foster has pursued a lifelong interest in the Threefold Social Order in study groups and as an author and sometime editor.

Rudi Lissau was a teacher at Wynstones Steiner School for forty years, and now writes and lectures.

Jenny Josephson practises medicine in Forest Row, East Sussex.